All Hell
Silas Hill – Book I

a supernatural thriller

by
Allan Burd

For more information on author:

www.allanburd.com

Cover art by Mark Roselle

ISBN: 0-9705588-2-1

ISBN-13: 978-0970558824

Box Nine Books

www.boxninebooks.com

1

My feet slip in the rain-slickened mud sending me tumbling end over end downhill. It's only by the grace of God that my thick skull doesn't crack like a walnut against the trees and boulders I roll by, though it would serve me right. Tonight, I was the textbook definition of fuck up with no one to blame but myself. Someone set me up. They pushed my buttons and I blindly jumped into their trap. I'll can kick myself in the ass later. Right now I just need to survive.

As soon as the ground levels out, I roll to my feet. It takes me less than a second to regain my orientation then I continue my mad dash through these unforgiving woods. Howls reverberate behind me like Mother Nature's sick way of ringing the dinner bell and the big joke is I can't run far enough or fast enough away to avoid being the feast. Forest's end is still a good mile away and even in the unlikely event I make it that far, the open fields that act as a buffer between these monsters and civilization will make me as easy to catch as a fish in a bowl.

I speed through the first-grade math in my head. Six of them against one of me equals I ain't gonna make it out of here alive. Not without one hell of a fight that the odds of me winning range from slim to no fucking way.

For the third time in the last ten minutes I take a mental inventory of my arsenal. I'm holding my Lupara double-barreled, sawed-off shotgun tight in my grip like a security blanket. I have eight extra shells, all custom filled with pure silver pellets, in my waist pocket. My Tomcat and Px4 Storm, fully loaded with my homemade 9mm wolf-killers, are snug to my left hip and right thigh. I've got seven additional magazines bouncing around in my backpack, along with the assortment of handheld weapons I bring every time I hunt. I don't think any of it is going to be enough. Not when all of them are on me at once.

I'm a vengeful enough bastard where I'll take a few of them with me, but in the end I'll go down just the same. They're too fast, too strong, and too vicious for me to get all of them before they eat all of me. I packed light. *Too light.*

I look around for an edge… some advantage I haven't yet noticed that might make all the difference between life and death. All I see is the same worn path through this dank, godforsaken forest that I saw on the way in. I'm vaulting a tree stump in front of me when I decide it's time to change course. Straight ahead is nothing more than a dead man's run, one I have no hope of surviving. I divert left, dart through the thicker, rougher terrain, and hope it changes my luck.

I slide my Lupara into the sheath sewed into my backpack then whip out the Storm and waste one round praying to get lucky. The empty silence that follows the shot mocks my desperation. I went off foolish, cocky, and now it is going to bite me in the ass… literally. I assumed I was dealing with a rogue, one lone wolf who strayed off the reservation, one sadistic prick of a werewolf who didn't abide by the rules and had a funny way of killing, ignoring that these monsters usually work in packs.

However, when I saw what it did to Old Man Jones, my thinking went awry. My logical side was run over by pure emotion, pure rage. It brought back memories, bad ones, and I went from smart to stupid faster than my Mustang goes from zero to ninety-five.

They howl again, six of them, one after the other in echoing waves that roll toward me like a collapsing row of dominos. I hit the brakes behind a fat oak and listen closely to the last cry, trying to calculate the distance between us. It's obvious they're close… minutes away, but I still can't spy them. Doesn't matter though.

I've had enough encounters with werewolves to know they've spied me. They have my scent. They aren't going to lose me. And they aren't going to settle for anything less than my meat and blood.

I sprint on as fast as my small stride and compact frame allow. A picture of my tombstone flashes through my mind: "Here lies Silas Hill. Short man. Short life." But if any of the mourners knew the shit I've seen and the things I've done, they'd put my balls in a mausoleum.

A row of brambles line in front of me and I quickly realize where I am… the ass end of Smithfield farms. The spiked blackberry bushes in front of me are imported from Asia and produce the finest berries in the county. Smithfield's makes a living selling them at a premium and they're worth it. Between those, picking pumpkins, and the hayrides, this place is one of the few, rare, fond childhood memories I have. My pa used to bring me and my brother here twice a month when we were kids. I still remember the layout pretty well. The stables are just a short distance away. Seems as good a place as any to make my last stand.

I slip between the bushes. The prickly thorns nip at my clothes. A sharp one rips through and gashes my left arm. I feel the liquid leak out of me and think the blood-covered blackberries will give the werewolves an appetizer, a delicious taste of what's to come. The stable looms large ahead of me, like a lighthouse to a lost sailor. It's old and rickety, as if the wind itself could knock it down. I plan to use it as a fortress. I race to its wooden doors and toss aside the two-by-four it uses as a door lock. The creaking alerts the horses who snort and clatter their hooved feet.

They're clearly unsettled, and I wonder if it's me or if they somehow sense the death I brought along. It dawns on me that this wasn't a good idea. It's not like I planned for it, but whatever I was thinking these poor horses weren't a part of it. Though, there's nothing I can do about it now. I'm about to slip inside when I see another option… or more accurately smell one.

To come out on top, the element of surprise is key. That means masking my scent. The manure pile is about five-feet high, which makes it taller than I am. There has to be at least a week's worth of horseshit there. Only two types of people I know who value shit this much; farmers, to fertilize their fields, and terrorist bomb makers, to fertilize their twisted ideals. I was about to be the third.

Aa I approach, the stench hit me like a punch in the nose. Nothing like a smattering of rain to keep manure fresh. At least the softness of it makes it easier to waddle into. I holster the Storm and redraw the Lupara then take a deep long breath. I keep the barrel down and my mouth shut so neither clog as I ease my way in, making sure every lovable inch of me is covered.

I'm in deep shit, first figuratively and now literally.

I always wanted to go out in style.

2

Ten seconds head-to-toe in shit and my thoughts drift back to what led me here. I was welcomed home by the smell of jack and vomit. My pa was comatose on the couch, snoring like a bull with too many rings in his nose. I tossed a blanket over him and tidied up around him. Then, just as I was settled in, the phone rang. It was Sheriff Martaan.

He wasn't expecting me to pick up, but he seemed more than okay with it. He told me we were the first call on his list. That jolted me. My pa's as big and tough as anyone, the guy you want on your side when you're in a situation. But he's also a short-tempered drunk who answers to no one but the corps. He's not first on anyone's list unless things are monstrous.

I told Martaan I'd be right there. I didn't need to say a word about my pa. Martaan knew us well enough to know that if I picked up, Pa was probably sleeping one off. The location he gave me wasn't too far away. I grabbed my slicker, my gear, and went for a stroll.

I could tell the scene was bad even before I got on top of it. Jones's old lady was wailin' up a storm in the arms of Larry, the local preacher, while the sheriff was shaking his head, hat in his lap, sitting on a stump off to the side. There was no one examining the body or the crime scene. We weren't just his first call… Martaan wanted one of us to be the first to see it. As I approached it, I immediately saw why.

Jones' body was laid out; arms spread wide, legs tight together, like our Lord and savior Jesus Christ hung out on the cross. He was gutted side to side, his innards spilling out like a deer being prepared for market. Three parallel gashes from ear to nose marked his right cheek. I knew I was going to find identical gashes on the other cheek even before I flipped his face over to look at the other side.

I backpedaled. Martaan called us because a monster did this. What he didn't know was it was also personal. Deeply personal. The way the body was left and the pattern of the wounds were identical to the ones that killed my brother. The only difference was that these claw marks were jagged while the one's that killed my brother were clean.

Martaan approached with a somber stride. He pointed to the lacerations. "Werewolves," he spat, "so much for the agreement."

His presence tempered my rage. He was afraid. Los Agros was werewolf country. They occupied the woods while we uprights occupied the valley. They don't bother us; we don't bother them. That's been the unwritten treaty for years. Tonight's murder changes that. I bent down and examined the wounds more closely. I couldn't find anything that disagreed with Martaan's conclusion. A werewolf definitely did this. The only question Martaan had was why. The more important question I had was why like this?

"Who else had access to the body?" I asked Martaan with a sharper edge in my tone than what's ordinarily there.

"No one," replied Martaan. "Mrs. Jones was right here when it happened. They were walking home when the beast struck out of nowhere. Killed him, just like that, one swipe across the gut. The spatter pattern confirms it. Though why he rearranged him like that and scratched his face the way he did baffles me. Larry and I heard Mrs. Jones screaming and ran out but the creature was long gone by then."

Mrs. Jones broke free of the Preacher, came barreling toward me. "You find it, Silas," she cried out. "You find that horror and you put it down. You kill it. Kill it dead." Her fist came down on my shoulder and she collapsed into me.

I'm four-foot-five and still people lean on me. But I understood. I didn't know Mr. Jones that well, but it's a small town so I knew him well enough. He was a decent man. He never did anything great, but he never did anything terrible either. Not so far as I know. He seemed a good husband and a good provider. He didn't deserve this. I held her, awkward as it was.

"You make it suffer too," she added, wiping her eyes, regaining her composure.

I looked her straight in the eye and gave her a slight nod, making it a promise I planned to keep. "Did you get a good look at it?" I asked her.

"I'll never forget it. It stared right at me when it put him like that… like it was rejoicing in my pain. Green glowing eyes, a scar under the left one, and a missing tooth. Dark brown coat, too."

"It's my problem, now," I told her. An officer draped a white sheet over the body, bringing a weird sense of finality to the whole thing. Though to me, it was just beginning. "I promise," I added. She seemed to accept that as she allowed Preacher Larry to throw his arm around her and remove her from the scene.

The brief exchange brought things into focus. I re-examined the body. There was no mistaking it. The marks were different but the same. I was going to track and kill the beast, not only for

Mrs. Jones, but also for myself. But first he was going to give me some answers. I studied the ground surrounding the body. Two wolf prints, both upright, followed by alternating patterns as it came and fled. The beast approached all wolf, went full *were* for the kill then turned back into a wolf for a quick exit. The ground was wet so the trail was easy to follow.

Rage bubbled within me. This thing had a lot to answer for. The sheriff wanted to know why it broke the truce, Mrs. Jones wanted revenge, and I needed to know what it had to do with the death of my brother. I told the sheriff I would hunt it tonight. He'd have enough on his plate trying to keep the townsfolk from full panic. The quicker we knew what was going on the better. I raced home, got what I thought I'd need, and returned.

"I'll be back in the morning with answers," I said to the Sheriff. "If not, well, that's an answer too."

"You don't want backup?" Martaan asked.

"You know I work alone. But be prepared to call in all of your reserves. This could be the brink of war."

I saw his adam's apple undulate before he steeled himself. Werewolves were nasty business that no one wanted a part of. "Damn, let's pray it's not. Good luck."

"Good luck to all of us," I responded.

I lowered my nose to the grindstone and followed the trail. The bastard made it easy, like he either had nothing to worry about or didn't care. Even so, once I hit the woods things got a little trickier. I had to be careful. I didn't want to encounter any werewolves other than this one. My hope was that the lone wolf wouldn't be going back to the den. I made sure I stayed downwind at all times.

Yet, something went wrong.

Though, as my eyes peer out from the manure pile, as I wait for the pack's imminent arrival, I still can't figure out what. I hear the howls again. They're louder and the echo drags on. They've moved into open space. I figure it'll be less than a minute til we see how this all pans out.

3

A minute's a long time when you're waiting for death. Given the line of work I'm in, I should have figured my last words would be with a monster.

I had tracked the lone werewolf for hours. Only once did his path cross with others of his kind and those tracks were a lot older. It convinced me more than ever I was dealing with a stray which was the best-case scenario. I just had to kill it and life in Los Agros would return to normal. The spacing and depths of its tracks told me it was close. I climbed a tree, found a perch, and scouted the area. There he was, lapping up lake freshwater not more than 20 yards away.

He made it easy. Killing him would've been a snap, but I needed him to talk. That meant wounding him enough so he couldn't fight back but not enough where he wouldn't feel obliged to chat. The crimson trace laser sighting on my Cat enabled me to shoot with the precision of a surgeon and the suppressor over the threaded barrel made the shots a silent operation.

I started with its right hind leg. The bullet sliced through its joint and anterior ligaments, almost completely severing its leg below the knee. It dropped with a muffled yelp. My next shot turned its front paw into pudding. It squirmed on the ground and tried to get away when I placed another in its ass to settle it down. Its time was up. The only question was whether its secrets would expire with it. I jumped to a lower branch then swung to the ground. Its green eyes glowed, just as Mrs. Jones said, and the scar ran longer than I imagined. I pressed the barrel of the Beretta against its floppy ear.

"Fuck you, Silas," said the wolf, with a snarl.

I was only mildly surprised the bastard knew who I was. I had a reputation, and this wasn't my first time in wolf country. "Glad you know me," I replied. "On the other hand, I couldn't give a shit to know you."

The wolf grimaced, more laughter than pain. "Well, ya ain't gonna forget me now."

Its teeth snapped at me. I pulled my arm away and cracked it on the side of the head with the Beretta. My bullets were made of silver. The handle of my gun was not. The blow hardly hurt it, but it got my message across. "Why'd you kill him?"

"That's the food chain, dipshit," he said.

I pushed the barrel into its ear. "Why like that?"

The wolf grimaced again. "Just sending a message. The old man made a good piece of paper."

"From whom?" I demanded.

"Someone who cares," he said, with a following growl.

"Are you going to get specific, or do I end this now?" I put a pound of pressure on the trigger, knowing it could hear the slight click.

Its green eyes locked with mine. "You really don't know. And I can't tell you." We both heard leaves rustle in the background. "Better hurry up and kill me now before you're deader than me," he added.

The fucker grinned and my eyes widened with the realization that I've been played. I heard a twig snap not too far away. Mr. Jones was more than a message. He was a lure. "Fuck!" I muttered.

Scarface was laughing so hard he started choking. It really pissed me off. I put a bullet in his brain and rabbited. They've been on my trail ever since.

Now I'm in deep shit and who knows how many pounds of it. I hear them snaking their way through the brambles despite what I'm covered in. I spit out, trying not to think about the crap that just crossed my lip.

I ready my Lupara.

The first one enters my field of view.

Everything I'm sitting in is about to hit the fan.

4

The full moon and open sky make it easy to see the death that comes my way. The pack leader has a coat of shiny brown fur that reflects the moonlight. He looks healthy and well fed which means he gets what he wants when he wants it. I mark him as the alpha dog and give even odds he's going to be the most dangerous. He whiffs the ground, nodding in the direction of the stables. Yeesh… he's the leader and the point man. In my head I call him Scout.

I have a habit of naming the monsters I encounter. Being a paranormal assassin is an inhuman business. I like to make it more personal. Behind Scout is a stocky wolf whose brown coat gives off a reddish cast. This one doesn't like to stay on all fours for too long, bouncing up frequently as he looks around. Jittery and red. I nickname him Fire. He overshadows the smaller wolf next to him. Nothing about that one stands out to me except for his size. He's little like me. Fuck him. He's Runt.

Three more round out their war party; a white one with a snarl you could crap your pants from, a big black one with a long scar across his snout, and a fat brownie who continually scratches his back. In my mind they're now Ivory, Ebony, and Fleas. Of the following five, the piano keys looked to be the strongest, but Fire is the one I'm most worried about. It's practically impossible to catch the nervous ones off guard and stealth is the only way I'm making it out of this alive.

Scout leads them to the stable door, sees it's slightly ajar. I didn't leave it like that on purpose, but if they figure I went inside instead of doubling back into this shit pile that's a helpful advantage. I angle the Lupara outward, pointing it in their direction. If they all go inside then I won't have to use it. I'll just retrace my trail and be home before they figure out how I got away. However, if they turn toward me, I'll at least take a few of the bastards with me.

Then Scout surprises me. He jumps up on his hinds and motions his hands like a military commander. Maybe that's what he was in his previous life, maybe not, but either way he knows his business. And even six-on-one, he isn't fucking around. He sends Fleas and Ebony around back to guard the rear door. After waiting a moment, he sends Fire around the side. Then he and Ivory enter the stable while Runt is left guarding the door.

I hear the horses whinny. The poor animals are fucked. I imagine their fear as I scroll through my own options. I could blow Runt to smithereens and make a mad dash but that would only grant me the minute it would take the other five to catch up to me. I could bolt now on the one-in-a-million chance that Runt, with his enhanced senses, won't hear me. Neither option is even mildly appealing so I stay put. Then Runt starts sniffing around. He picks up my double back and eyes the shit pile I'm in like he's struck gold. He approaches, cautiously. I'm royally fucked, but so is he.

He's only a foot away, his eyes scanning everywhere. He's recoiling from the smell, unable to confirm my scent through the overwhelming stench. The manure covers me well. He has no idea I'm right in front of him. I could see the wheels turning behind those angular yellow eyes. He knows I'm in here, but he isn't overly eager to come in and find me. I decide to make his life easier. But only for the split second it takes me to end it.

I step out. "What's the matter? You don't like shit on your food." Then I pull the trigger, letting loose two buckshots filled with pure silver pellets that explode his head like a dropped watermelon.

Now things are going to happen fast. Gunfire has that way of alerting people. I don't even have the chance to shake the shit off me before Ebony and Fleas round the corner. I quickly ditch my Lupara and reach for the Bobcat. They're charging equal parts velocity and ferocity. I raise the Cat and charge back. My first shot severs Fleas front right leg. He face plants and my aim is already on my next mark. I use Ebony's scar as a target and put two rounds in his face. His head snaps back as his body slides forward at my feet. I'm pretty sure he's dead, but when I'm facing life ending situations I tend to get a little anal. I put another round in Ebony's gut as I jump over him. Fleas is trying to get up. I give him a permanent cure for his itch by pumping three into him as I run past.

I don't miss a stride as I reach my destination, a dumpster on the side of the stable that makes a good first step on my climb to the roof. There are still three left. I need the high ground but my height disability is making this a challenge. I roll atop the dumpster easy enough, but my arms can't reach the roof. A pipe is sticking out of the rotted wall. I grab it and pull myself high enough to gain a foothold on the windowsill. From there, I swing my other hand up and grip the ledge pulling myself all the way up, but the extra time it takes cost me.

I wasn't the only one who understood the advantage of high ground. Scout knew it as well. He hadn't sent Fire around the side like I first thought. He sent him up on the roof. The jittery bastard was his best lookout. Now instead of me getting the drop on them, Fire's got the drop on me. I plant my knee, and roll to my back as he pounces. I get off one shot before he's on top of me, knocking the gun from my hand and driving my shoulders into the cheap thin wood. Aside from his berries, Smithfield's known for one other thing. He's a cheap bastard. He only took care of the things that made him money. The stable roof wasn't one of them.

The rickety untreated wood cracks beneath our weight and buckles. We plunge the fifteen feet to the sounds of dilapidation and wild horses. I land in a pile of hay, a vast improvement from the last pile I lay in. Must've been god's way of evening things out. Fire's fall, and his back, break against the topside of a stall. He probably would've healed from it quick enough had he not already been dead. The shoot I got off was a lucky one. Black cherry blood oozes out of his chest as he hangs there like a fur coat on a drying line. My bullet hit him right in the heart. His eyes still look at me, though they are as dead now as much as they were alive when he thought he had me.

My guns are saving my ass tonight. I reach for the last one I have, my Storm, only to find it missing. It must have dropped when I fell. I search the haystack beneath me. It isn't like looking for a needle, but still, I'm not going to have time to look. The horse in the stall we dropped into is bucking wildly and I hear growls from both sides of me. I'm boxed in with nowhere to go.

A horse two stalls away let out a long neigh. I see its front two hooves high in the air then hear a sickening wail and a crunch as it drops to the floor. The smell of fresh intestines hit the air hard enough to overpower the manure that is still caked all over me. I hear another death cry followed by the increased intensity of horseshoes on the ground as fear runs wild. Scout and Ivory are turning this stable into a slaughterhouse and I'm the cream filling.

5

My only chance is to take them on one at a time hand-to-hand. There isn't a man alive that could take one of these beasts in a fair fight, let alone a little guy like me. Fortunately, I never fight fair.

I dump the contents of my backpack, ignoring the chaos of stomps and snarls all around me. My assortment of small weapons spill out but I'm only interested in one, a pair actually. I immediately find them, slip my fingers through the eight rings, and clasp my fist around them with my free thumbs. My hands are now wrapped in spiked metal bands with daggers that extend out to the side, all made of pure silver. They're worth a pretty penny on the open market. Worth a helluva lot more to me now. They make the ordinary brass knuckles I have at home look like a child's toy. Still, I'll need more to even the odds.

I scoop up my canteen. Most survivalists like myself fill their canteens with water. They don't face the same hazards I do. Mine contains gasoline. I flip open the top and pour fuel on Fire. I grab a matchbook, scrape one stick then fold it in on itself lighting up the entire package. I toss it onto the dead werewolf, inwardly chuckling at the irony of the nickname I gave him as his fur bursts into flames. This evening's been a smorgasbord of the worst smells known to mankind and I just added burnt hair and charred flesh to the menu.

My head is on a swivel. I expected Ivory or Scout to be on me by now. So far they've been cautious, content in just killing everything around me. I can only guess they're afraid of the guns they don't know I lost and are killing the horses to draw me out into the open. Another horse screams his death knell and it's like a knife to my stomach. I brought the wolves to their door. Now the horses are paying the price. I light up another matchbook and toss it at the sound of the most recent death. It lands on a hay pile and immediately catches. The horse will get a Viking funeral, which has to be preferable to being devoured by wolves, and hopefully it will cause Scout and Ivory to think twice before they kill another one. I throw the entire canteen there for extra measure.

With one side of me aflame and smoke filling the air, it's time to make my move. I lift the bar, freeing the poor palomino stuck with me. As he makes his mad dash for freedom, I stay low beneath the fumes to get a better view at the situation. I see

Scout's furry legs to my left, retreating outside. To my right, the rear doors are pushed wide open thanks to the horse that raced through them. I head in that direction, opening up every stall on the way. Two black beauties leap out in front of me and flee to fresh air. Behind me my canteen pops, invigorating the burn. I bolt toward the exit, but something bolts faster.

It's Ivory bursting through one of the gates. Chunks of wood splinter in every direction then he's right there, his fangs going straight for my throat. I get three spikes through his jaw before he has the chance to snap down. His tainted blood dances on my fingers as he skids off to the side. I hurt him but not nearly enough. He turns on a dime, shows me the teeth he's going to use to end my life.

Our eyes lock. I stare him down, directly challenging his dominance, and position myself in an offensive stance. He doesn't care. We both know he's coming in for the kill. I bring my arm up, dagger out in front. He lunges, coming at me claws first. I sidestep and twist to simultaneously avoid him and slash outward. I'm only half successful. My blade slices the paw closest to me but the other hits me hard and knocks me back sending me tumbling beneath the smoke. The flames lick my back.

I quickly remove my coat as it catches fire and toss it at Ivory. It pillows out, falling well short, creating a bonfire that both of us circle around. I can see him thinking about clearing it in one jump. It would be easy enough for him, but it would bring him too close to the inferno. Besides, I'm the one pinned down. The next move has to be mine. I have three choices; circle around to the right, circle to the left, or burn. I choose right, eyeing a large piece of wood that lay there. I snatch it then light it up in the bonfire like a torch and swing it in front of me, momentarily keeping Ivory at bay. It's a desperate play that will only last the time it takes the board to burn to cinders in my hand.

"Go home," I order him. "We both know fire and werewolves don't mix."

He grins. "Hell Pack likes the heat."

I don't know what Hell Pack means. Guess that's what they call themselves but I'm not going to ask. The time for talk is over. The fire is eating up the board, threatening to singe my fingertips. It's time to get wet. I throw the fiery remains at him, forcing him left, and lunge in with my knives. My first slash misses by a mile. He slashes back, grazing my ribs enough to draw blood. But I'm too pumped up on adrenaline and fear to let that stop me.

Before his front quarter pulls back I punch through it with a spike. His jaw snaps forward. I arch back and slash forward cutting his snout. A claw slices through my cheek. I don't let myself feel it. I'm in pure panic mode. My ferocity has to equal his. I stop fighting, even for one second, and I die. I stab down. My blade pierces his shoulder. He picks me up and slams me to the ground. I react by throwing my left hand up. My dagger pierces his belly. He yelps. His fangs come for my face. I twist the knife, making him momentarily recoil as I really give him something to howl about. Silver works best when it stays on the inside so I leave it in place.

His jaw comes at me again. I roll beneath him as his fangs tangle with my hair. I thrust my other blade toward his heart. Something gushes. His fangs scrape my forehead and suddenly I'm in his mouth. His breath is hot and fetid and I'm surprised I have the time to notice it. My arms push him away, and I go into a stabbing frenzy, plunging my knife everywhere and anywhere until I realize he's already dead even before I pushed my way out of his mouth.

I'm scratched, bloodied, exhausted, and Ivory's saliva coats my skull. The pain I ignored comes forth with a vengeance. My senses are on overload as I try to regain control from the blind panic that overcame me. I breathe, thankful for the primal instinct that runs in my family that tells us to fight on, even one second past the moment we're dead. Smoke fills my eyes and lungs. Heat washes over me, warning me I can't remain here for long. I look down at the mess I made and reclaim my knives. There's still one big problem ahead of me. One I'm in no condition to take on. *Scout.*

Over half the stable is now consumed and the fire's hunger is growing fast. In the few seconds I have, I sort through the situation. Setting the fire may have cut off a double attack, but it limits me to only one avenue of escape, a severe tactical disadvantage. Watching Scout in action, I'm certain he's already picked up on that. I have one place to go and he's gonna be there waiting for me. He is the trap and I'm the mouse. The moment I step out, the moment he sees it's me and not Ivory, he's going to chomp down on me hard.

The only question is, which direction will he come at me from? *Hell Pack likes the heat.*

I immediately know.

Still, I'm only going to get one shot. I tighten my fist, making sure the silver knuckles are firmly in my grasp and dip my blades in the flames… a hot knife through butter and all that. Then I run like the north wind through the stable doors out into the night. My peripheral vision sees all clear to my left and right. Straight ahead I see the lights turn on in the Smithfield house in the distance. But I don't see Scout. That means I'm right.

I immediately pivot, whipping both my arms around in as high and wide an arc as I have, praying that I created enough space for me to get fully around in time. I see his golden eyes, practically on top of me. An instant later I feel the spurt as both my blades enter his throat.

His body collapses on mine.

The air shoots out of my lungs.

His blood puddles over me.

Then everything goes black.

6

I come to, but don't move. Laying here quietly with Scout seems like the only smart choice. My eye catches the back ledge of the stable, the perch where Scout waited for me. Flames crackle around it like a log in a fireplace. It's romantic. A starry night sky, a fire, and me lying next to the thing I love more than anything else in the world… a monster. I chortle til the pain no longer lets me.

"Hey," a voice screams in the distance, repeating like a stuck record. I tilt my head back and see Mr. Smithfield running toward me as fast as a man of his age can. He has a rifle in his hand. Then he halts in his tracks, catches a good eyeful of something, and flees back to his house as if he's seen a thousand ghosts.

"Fuck. What now?" I mutter. I stare into Scout's dead eyes as his vacant orbs stare back as if I should feel guilty about what I've done. "Fuck you." I kiss him on the nose then boot him off of me and get up, my joints snapping and cracking with every little movement. I think about dusting myself off, but between the shit, blood, and guts I don't want to sully my hands.

Something scared the shit off of Smithfield. Maybe they can do it for me too.

I'm on my feet, facing what's to come. I chuckle. All I can think of is that God fucking hates me. There has to be at least twenty of them… twenty more nasty fucking werewolves, marching in lock step like they were Army. I don't bother to run. I wait for them to come to me. I want the satisfaction of seeing the looks on their stupid faces when they see what I did to their friends. If war is coming, they'll know I won the first battle. Even if it's my last, they'll know I kicked their ass.

The pack stops, all except their leader, a large silver bastard I'd recognize anywhere who comes closer to me than my prom date. I met him before and call him Silver Joe. I was never sure if our relationship was one of mutual respect or mutual hate. He smells me and recoils. He takes in the burning stable, the scent of death, and the blood that's pooled around the carcass I named Scout.

He turns, issuing silent orders to his pack. A few break off toward what's left of the horse house. A black one comes forward. It gives me the stink eye then flings Scout's body over its shoulder and carries him away, a trail of blood following. Silver Joe never takes his eyes off of me the whole time.

"How many?" he snarls.

"Six," I answer. "Seven if you count the prick that started it." I spit. Equal parts blood and saliva hit the ground. "I don't get back by morning, this is just the beginning," I threaten.

I could see the hatred building behind his seasoned eyes. We stare each other down. He takes my full measure. I take his. Now I know our relationship. It's mutual hatred. His paw strikes like lightning across my head. My last thought is regret that the war will go on without me.

7

They say your life flashes before your eyes right before you die. My horror show starts with the first time I met Silver Joe.

It was the day my brother died… or more accurately thirteen hours after he was viciously slaughtered by something supernatural. I'd spent the afternoon in shock. By nightfall, I needed an outlet for my irrepressible rage. They were all the same to me back then. A monster was a monster. My pa said a monster killed him, I vowed to kill a monster in return. I grabbed my pa's rifle and night vision goggles and headed out into the woods. Whatever treaty we had with the werewolves be damned. Consequences were an afterthought… I was getting some revenge.

I was always a naturally good hunter, but at the time I was fueled by hate, not thinking clearly… a powder keg ready to explode, woefully ignorant of the true power of the paranormal forces that occupy our world. I came across some paw prints and tracked a small pack of werewolves deep into their territory. I found an advantageous position and spied four of them feasting on a deer like it was Thanksgiving dinner. Two of them stayed on all fours, like real wolves. The other two walked on their hinds like they were half-human.

Four monsters for my brother. It didn't feel like an even exchange—my brother was worth a thousand of them—but it was sure better than just an eye for an eye. I ran my scope over all of them, getting a good close look at the hideous beasts. One had a real stupid expression on his face, like a hyena. Another was making a mess of things, spitting deer guts everywhere as he plunged his snout in and out of Bambi then howled with his mouth full. One of the uprights had long fur. Another had a belly so big he resembled a bear more than wolf. I named 'em the fuck brothers; Dumb Fuck, Sloppy Fuck, Hairy Fuck, and Fat Fuck, but they were all dead fucks to me.

I lined up Fats in my sight, centering my target directly on that oversized stomach of his for no particular reason other than he was standing tall and I wanted to splatter his guts all over the others. With the butt of my gun in the pocket of my shoulder, I carefully took aim. My finger tightened on the trigger. Then they all turned toward me at once. It took me a split second to realize they knew I was there the whole time.

Something I didn't even see knocked the rifle from my grasp. Something sharp ripped across my thigh, involuntarily dropping me to one knee. Claws lashed out of nowhere, digging parallel gashes into my shoulder. I turned in time to see the finishing blow. A jet black werewolf with piercing orange eyes, standing on his hinds like a human, his fist curled in a ball of fur, landed a haymaker right across my face. I fell like one of Mike Tyson's opponents, a tooth of mine hitting the ground a second before my head did.

Through a fog I saw the five of them surrounding me. The fat one's drool dripped on my face. "Dessert," it said.

"No," growled the black one. "Bring him."

A dark hairy paw with a vise-like grip latched onto my ankle. My head bounced on the dirt as I was dragged through the woods leaving a trail of my blood behind me. I went in and out of consciousness until the ride finally stopped. I was tossed head first into a clearing, the dirt and wet grass caking against the side of my face as I landed. Snarls, growls, and howls echoed all around me as if I was grand prize in their victory parade.

Slowly, I rose to my feet, dizzily taking in the landscape in hopes of finding an exit strategy. Behind me lay the dark forest, two wolves standing guard. In front of me was the crowd. They easily numbered over fifty, a sea of angular glowing eyes and triangular teeth. A series of caves stood behind them. This must have been the main entrance to their den.

A large silver one, taller and more powerful looking than all the others, stepped forward, staring me down, appraising my worthlessness. I could tell all it wanted to do was rip me apart. "You are free. Go home," he snarled.

"Fuck you," was my brilliant reply.

He came closer, teeth bared, all serious business. "I am aware of your recent loss, Silas Hill. It was not our doing. Go now… before this becomes something *more*." It didn't take a genius to get his meaning. He looked ready to pounce the second I said no.

I paused for a moment, regaining my senses to the point I didn't feel vengeful or dumb enough to give him that no. But I wasn't ready to give him a yes either. He knew me. He just didn't know what an incorrigible prick I could be when I was mad. I decided to educate him. "What should I call you?" I asked.

"You ignorant little fuck," he growled, his teeth so close to me now I could see the remnants of his last meal stuck between his canines.

"That's kind of a long name," I retorted. "How about I call you Joe? Better yet, Silver Joe. You look like a Joe and you're silver." I grinned like a wise ass.

His hand immediately grabbed my throat, his claws scratching my skin, a warning of things to come if he decided to add a little more pressure. I grabbed his outstretched arm but it was useless. He was far too strong. Still, I didn't give a shit.

"Bring me the asshole that killed my brother or, I fucking swear, I will kill you," I threatened.

He growled, nearly putting my head in his mouth. "For the last time, *not* us," he said, his grip tightening, cutting off my air. "And I fucking swear, if you do not leave right now, I will remove your larynx and gut you for my pack."

His claws caressed my belly with enough pressure to make his point. My eyes tightened. So did his grip. He drew some of my blood just to emphasize his point.

"Believe me or die," he snarled.

It was an ultimatum I daren't refuse. I nodded and he released me, dropping me to the ground.

"Tell your father… tell Jebediah… he owes me one for sparing you." He howled at the moon, watching me intently as I left stumbling into the woods, the wolf guards sneering at me as I passed them by. I gave them the finger so they'd remember me. I'm charming that way and I don't deal well with losing. It took me hours to find my way home, days for the town doc to properly clean my wounds.

That was years ago when I was nothing more than a backwater hillbilly from this shithole town in the middle of the nowhere, USA. Having Silver Joe get the better of me again isn't exactly how I envisioned my homecoming.

8

I come to for long enough a moment to realize that dying isn't in the cards. I'm in too much freakin' pain. Around me throaty growls and inhuman voices whir by like a passing train. My eyes reveal only the blurriest of movements. Then I black out again and my freak show continues.

My brother is laid out lifeless on a sled. A coat covers his body. My pa had just dragged him from wherever they've been to the front steps of our church. Pa was pale, his face a portrait of loss painted with lines of sadness and regret. His eyes blank as if his soul had just been ripped out.

Mom knew immediately. She ran down the street, my father intercepting her, holding her tight, preventing her from looking too closely at my brother's body. I never heard exactly what they said to each other—I was too stunned, fixated on my brother's vacant bloodied face—but Ma was yelling something fierce, as if it were all Pa's fault. My brother... whatever killed him was animal-like, but there was something ritualistic about it too. Three parallel gashes lined each of his cheeks, the wounds too symmetrical for him to have been killed by any of the local wildlife.

The way my brother's eyes stared blankly into the heavens was like a dead fish unexpectedly pulled from the water. My brother was terrified before he died, so whatever got him had to be something that surprised him in the worst way, cause my brother knew the woods and everything that lived in it better than anybody. I never thought about it until now, but it was odd that my pa left his eyes open like that instead of simply closing them. An awful smell led me to peek under the coat and I caught a glimpse of my brother's inner workings before my father yanked me away.

An elder priest I've rarely had contact with appeared at the main entrance. It was Father Miguel. His hair was brittle white. He looked strong as an ox and his eyes were as powerful as God's. "Bring him around back," he ordered, soft but firm, as if he had already known what had happened and could provide a measure of comforting support. My father nodded and did as he was told, sending my mother home to grieve alone. I stood there, not sure which parent to follow. After about a minute, I chose to follow my brother.

I gently opened the back door to the church. It was an inner sanctum painted mostly white, sparsely decorated with religious ornaments. My brother was laid out on the bare floor in the exact position my father brought him in on the sled, except his arms were spread wide. "This is exactly how I found him," I overheard my pa say.

Father Miguel inspected the body. His fingers graced the lacerations on his face, tracing the cut lines. He studied the more severe wound to his belly, carefully inspecting inside my brother with a latex gloved hand. He shook his head, a sorrowful gesture before gently closing my brother's eyes. Then he drew a cross on his chest while looking upward toward God. When he finished his prayer, a solemn look defining his strong face, he said, "I am familiar with this."

"No," my father cried.

"You couldn't have known. It's not your fault," replied Miguel, placing his hand on my pa's shoulder.

"His soul?" my father pleaded.

"Beyond my ability to know. I will pray for it." Miguel paused. "I will locate the monster that did this."

"Impossible," my father frowned.

Miguel's expression was a mix of understanding and disappointment. "They work their evil in many ways. I will do what I can," he said.

I'm pushed from my memory as warm liquid splashes my face and gets in my mouth. I spit it out so I don't choke. I'm conscious, alive… awake. My eyes burn. I wipe them and see the familiar clearing in the woods. I'm once again at the entrance of the wolf's den. A campfire flickers nearby, giving off light and heat. I smell the urine as my confusion fades.

The black wolf's rear leg returns to the ground. "The little asshole's awake now," he snickers. His piercing orange eyes gaze through me and I recognize him immediately. It's déjà vu.

Silver Joe comes into my field of view. He's standing upright, looking intimidating and strong. His scraggily paw grips me by the hair as he lifts me painfully to my feet. "Welcome back, Silas," he says with a shit-eating grin.

Now I know where I am and how I got here. I can't wait to find out why they kept me alive.

9

"You look good, Silas," says the black werewolf.

I don't need to look in a mirror to get the sarcasm. I'm still caked in blood, guts, and horseshit and now I'm damp with warm werewolf piss as well. "Bite me," I retort.

"Later," he replies with a sneer.

My attitude doesn't bother him at all. He's seen it before. I notice the way he defers to Silver Joe and gather he's his right-hand man. I never gave him a nickname the last time we met. Today, in my head, I call him Sidekick.

I look to Silver Joe and say, "I'm still breathing. Why?"

He stares past me. Now that he's pummeled me there's a lot less hate in his eyes. "There are other forces at play," he says.

I quickly run through all the scenarios in my head. What he says make sense. Otherwise, I wouldn't have any meat left on my bones. "You could've told me that before you clocked me."

Sidekick snorts. "He could have, but I can tell you from experience that punching you in the face is just too much fun."

Joe hates me because I've given him reason to. Sidekick, on the other hand, is just a dick. I ignore him. There's something larger brewing here. I need to know what it is and what it might have to do with my brother's murder. I turn to Silver Joe with a look that requests an explanation.

"This is werewolf territory. You should have brought the matter immediately to my attention," he says, as if the matter wasn't cold-blooded murder. "Sneaking onto our land was… *disrespectful.*"

I make a mental note that he only mentioned *sneaking* was disrespectful. It was as if he somehow considered it a lesser offense than killing seven of his pack. "I had no way of knowing it wasn't an isolated incident," I reply calmly.

"You escalated things," answers Joe.

"One of yours crossed the line first," I say.

We stare at each other. An invisible mental chess match being played between us. I'm never going to acquiesce to any fault. Joe's never going to accept anything less than his dominance. But while I admire his thinking and his veneer of calm, Sidekick's wearing his heart on his sleeve. I can tell he wants to rip off my face just because he can. Silver Joe raises a paw holding him back.

"Not one of ours. An *outsider.* A few months back a wolf with green eyes appeared on our land. He lived among us without truly becoming one of us. He wasn't interested in making friends. In fact, just the opposite." Joe tilted his head toward a stocky wolf circling the campfire. It had an unseemly long scar that ran from its rib cage to the base of its skull, an unnatural part in its brown fur. "He carved out a small territory for himself along the outskirts. He was a tough hombre. I saw no need for unnecessary bloodshed. We came to an understanding. If he was content to play the lone wolf, I would allow it, as long as he didn't cause any trouble. He never officially agreed to it, but he never disagreed with it either, so we let him be."

Joe paused. I caught a glimmer of anger in his eyes as the flame from the campfire reflected in his pupil. I just couldn't tell for whom. Joe continued. "But others in our clan did not. Six brother wolves began following his movements. At first, it was out of curiosity. They studied him. Then they liked what they saw. This lone wolf didn't bother any of us, but he didn't follow our rules either. He went wherever he pleased. They respected that. They believed obeying my rules made us weak. Then, a few days ago, they followed him to the graveyard."

The graveyard. Just the mention of that place sent a chill up my spine. The graveyard was a hub for some of the nastiest, most vile creatures that ever walked the face of the earth. Long ago, it was dubbed forbidden territory. Even the werewolves didn't go there. Until now…

"When they returned, they started referring to themselves as Hell Pack. I should've killed them all the moment I heard that," says Joe.

"Seems to me then that I took care of a problem for you," I say.

Joe snarls. "It wasn't your problem to deal with."

"I was hoping to avert a war."

"Still, an outsider killing our kind creates a problem. There are those among us, who, even despite knowing the circumstances, will hunger for payback."

"Yet here I sit in the middle of your dinner table. A dish served cold," I say.

Silver Joe pauses, lost in thought. "Follow me, Silas." He trots into a nearby cave. Sidekick goes in right behind him. I stare down the gauntlet of angry, untrusting glares that eye me with hatred and follow them both inside.

The surprises keep coming. I expect an empty cave. Instead, inside is a combination family living room and local gun exhibit. Along the stone wall to my right is a rifle rack, its storage capacity maxed out. A quick peruse gives me a count of twenty weapons from at least six different gun manufacturers. Some look over ten years old, worn from use. A Ruger Mini 14 looks cleaner than the rest. It's almost brand new and stands out like a sore thumb.

Next to the rack is a white clothed-covered table on top of which is a variety of handguns. I eye the lot of them, eyeing a .44 Magnum, a Sig Sauer, and a Glock 19… then my glance fixates on a second-generation Colt single action revolver. It had to be over 60 years old. I pick it up, flip it side to side, give it a close inspection. It's in excellent condition save for a few grooves that run along the barrel. I comment. "Where'd you get this?"

Silver Joe looks back at me. "Same place we get them all… from those foolish enough to hunt us."

Sidekick pulls a rifle from the rack. "Recognize this, asshole?"

I'll be damned. It was my pa's. The one I grabbed when I went off half-cocked after my brother's death to lay waste to some of these bastards.

He re-racks it. "You can't have it back. I like to think of it as a trophy of mine. Finders' keepers and all that." Sidekick grabs a

Smith & Wesson SD9 off the table and tosses it to me. "This one you can play with. Ammo for it is in the third draw," he says, tilting his head toward a beat up wooden cabinet which hugs the left wall of the cave.

"Did the hunters come after you with furniture too?" I ask.

"No, but they carried American Express," says Sidekick.

I chuckle. I can't help myself. The asshole actually made me laugh. "I hope you used it better than just buying this piece of shit. Where'd you shop, Ikea?" I open the draw and see an impressive array of ammunition. There has to be ammo here for every different weapon that they captured. And plenty of it too. Only me and my pa had more. "Holy shit," I mutter.

"Membership has its privileges," says Silver Joe.

I picture werewolves walking into a gun store. Doesn't seem plausible. So, either some of these guys can revert back to full human or they have human runners. More likely the latter. I grab a few boxes of 'nines' suitable for the Smith & Wesson. "Anything in silver?"

Silver Joe shoots me a look that could kill. I shrug. The guy spared my life and here I was, being a prick. Of course, there wasn't going to be any silver ammunition. At least not here. I don't yet know why they're arming me, but they certainly aren't stupid enough to give me something I might use against them.

Silver Joe opens another draw. He pulls out an iPhone 5 and tosses it to me. "Call whoever you're supposed to. Tell them to stand down. We are not at war."

"Well, fuck me, a werewolf with a cell phone. Now I've seen everything. Kinda gives a whole new meaning to call of the wild. Do you use Sprint or AT&T?"

"Do you want to be at war with us?" says Joe, tiring of my shit.

I tap the phone and get a dial tone. "You get reception out here. Well, fuck me twice." I start dialing.

"Tell 'em you won't be back as planned either," Sidekick says, before I finish pressing all the digits.

That got my panties in a bunch. "Why? You gonna kill me after I make the call?" I ask, staring intently into his eyes for the real answer.

"Not directly after. Another time," Sidekick answers, approaching me, glaring back at me with the intensity of the killing machine that he is.

Silver Joe steps between us. He looks at me. "We don't want there to be any *misunderstandings*. You're going to head straight for the graveyard," he says. "That's why we're giving you guns. You'll need to be able to defend yourself against what you'll find." Then he turns to Sidekick, "And you're going to escort him there." Joe steps back but speaks again before either of us could protest. "We know the land better as well as the dangers that lurk and I don't want any of our kind getting in your way. On your own, you're as good as dead. Together, you'll get there safely and we need to know what's going on as well."

Silver Joe knew me well. If this started because some lone wolf went to the graveyard, I had to check it out and make sure whatever threat exists there is dealt with. I also strongly suspect the answer to why Old Man Jones was laid out like my brother will be there as well. I nod. I look at Sidekick. "Well, look at that… you're my official tour guide."

"I'll get you there. But I'm not bringing you back," Sidekick snarls. Joe snarls louder and Sidekick gives in. "Fine… you're going to need more than the pistol. Load up. Anything but what was once yours."

I go to the rifle rack. I reach for my pa's then as Sidekick reacts to my gesture I flip him the bird and grab the Rugen, using the strap to sling it over my shoulder. My pa's rifle could wait for another day. Next, I rummage through the draw and grab its matching ammo, along with a few more additional magazines for the SD9. I open the draw below it and see a selection of knives and other sharp hand-held weapons. But, unfortunately, not the ones I came in with. They stripped me of those before they woke me and must've hid them elsewhere. I grab two daggers, an axe, and put a machete in my belt. Then I go back to the gun table and grab the Colt. I don't need any ammo for it. I have no plans to use it. Once this is over I'm going to sell it. A second generation, in as good condition as this one, is worth around a cool ten grand.

10

I call Sheriff Martaan and tell him I'm as okay as Wyatt Earp at the Corral. Only he and I know what that really means. I give him the rest of the sitrep, hearing the relief in his voice as I do, then Sidekick and I are off to grandma's house. The other wolves are glaring at us. They look mean, but they always look like that so I can't read their true intentions. Doesn't matter. With Sidekick next to me they leave me alone.

We hit the woods, the light of the full moon piercing its way through the treetops enough where I can see my way. I figure the graveyard's about a two-mile hike so I decide to make some small talk. "So, where are you from?" I ask, like we're two travelers randomly meeting on vacation.

"What the fuck is that supposed to mean?" replies Sidekick.

"I mean originally. What were you in your previous life? Before you were this. Before you were bitten," I ask.

"Bitten?" He snorts. It was a guffaw, yet with the throaty growl of a wolf. "You have no idea where werewolves come from, do ya?" he adds, trotting ahead of me as if I was insignificant.

I could tell his opinion of me dropped a notch. Not hatred wise—he hated me worse than anyone could—but knowledge wise. He thought I was smarter. But he was right. Other than knowing how to kill them, I really didn't know much about 'em. Maybe werewolves weren't turned by being bitten. Still, he was pissing me off and I never properly paid him back for pissing on me.

His arrogant rump was a few yards ahead of me. I think about testing the accuracy of the SD9, plugging him one where the sun don't shine. But no silver meant he'd heal in seconds and I don't cherish the thought of him returning the favor. He wasn't looking at me. I could ditch him too—I knew I couldn't fully trust him—but Silver Joe put me in a smart box. If there were other wolves out to get me, or other things that Sidekick knew about that I didn't, Sidekick was my best chance for survival. The enemy of my unknown enemy was momentarily my friend. Any petty revenge I could plan would have to wait.

I catch up to him like a puppy running to follow its mommy. "So, no one ever bit you?" I ask, figuring I might as well learn more.

He chuckles. "When one of us bites you, we don't leave anything big enough left to live. We're at the top of the food chain. It's the natural order of things." He smirks.

Okay, I think. "But before… before you were someone, someone human?"

"Some of us remember. Some of us don't. Some of us don't care to. All I know is before I was like this, I was like you… *weak*."

This conversation is going nowhere. I clam up and we walk for a while in silence. When we reach the edge of his territory, I start to prepare. I check the guns making sure the barrels are clear, spinning and clicking the mechanisms to be certain they aren't going to jam on me at an inopportune moment. Everything appears to be in working order. I lock and load all but the Colt and make sure the handhelds are easily accessible in case the need arises.

"Things are going to start getting interesting," says Sidekick.

My senses go on high alert. I constantly scan my 360. About 20 yards to my left, I spot a grey rabbit bouncing around. I jam the butt of the Ruger into the pocket of my shoulder and line it up in the square of the crosshairs.

"I wouldn't," warns Sidekick.

"Why not? Am I taking your breakfast?" My finger is on the trigger, but I'm not going to shoot it. I'm not big on killing the innocent. Instead, I look for a spot a few feet to the left of him I can use as a bullseye, a place where I can test the accuracy of the weapon then watch the bunny skitter off. Then something funny about the rabbit catches my eye… a glimmer of the fading moonlight reflecting off his face. I zoom in with the scope. Not his face… *his front teeth.* Two mini buck fangs are protruding out of the center of its mouth. It sees me and snarls and I'm shit sure not looking at the Easter Bunny. This wasn't Brer Rabbit. This was were-rabbit.

It darts toward me, the complete opposite of what a normal rabbit would do. I fire a round but its movements are quick and dart-like. The bullet splashes the ground, kicking up the dirt a few feet behind where it just was. The sucker can move. I reacquire him about ten yards from me, coming in fast. I immediately recognize the zigzag pattern of attack from my years of hunting predators, anticipate his next move, and place a bullet in its midsection that shreds its gut. But it doesn't even slow down. He lands, pushes off his back legs and, just like that, his teeth are a foot away from my throat. With no time for another shot, I swing the rifle like a baseball bat. I miss by a country mile. Then a furry black hand snatches it out of the air an inch in front of my face.

"Cute little fella," says Sidekick, watching it wildly snap its buck teeth within his fist. Then he squeezes it tight until it stops struggling and bites its head off. "Not very tasty though." He spat it out as he said the words. "The closer we get, the more unnatural fun like this we'll encounter. Try to stay alive. I want the pleasure of killing you for myself."

His eyes light up as he says it. He's enjoying this, the crazy fuck. And he's warning me about 'unnatural' things as if he's the natural one. I scan the immediate area. A white rabbit is sitting there off to my right, this one missing half its face. One of its eyes is popped out, hanging loosely over the muscle tissue on its jaw. A large section of its yellow-hued skull is exposed showing off its back teeth, a complete row of mini fangs that would make a piranha jealous. *Zombie were-rabbits.* This was Alice Cooper in Wonderland, but I had no interest in following this furry fuck down his rabbit hole. Sidekick tosses the headless rabbit body he was holding at it. It takes the hint and scurries off.

I pick up some wolf prints ahead of me. A quick inspection shows me different lengths and different depths. In the mud, I spot a brown strand with a reddish cast. It had to have belonged to Fire. "Hell Pack's been here. They went this way." I nod in the proper direction and Sidekick follows, though I'm beginning to feel that he wasn't anyone's sidekick. In fact, I'm pretty sure I'm his.

We walk for a bit. Some scratches in a tree catch my eye. One of Hell Pack must've marked it on the way… probably without even thinking about it. I hear a faint hiss and glance up. Sidekick's leaning against a tree. Above him, a snake is slithering down for the kill. I pull out a dagger, fling it with expert accuracy, and it plunges through the head of the snake just as it's about to strike, pinning it to the tree right beside Sidekick's neck. Yet, despite the sharp blade through its brain, it's still flailing around like a stuck pig. I'm amazed. Here we were next to a graveyard and nothing seems to die.

"You're welcome," I say.

"Wasn't a concern," says Sidekick, just as another snake whips at him from above. Without looking, Sidekick reaches up and crushes its head in his paw. "Nice to see you care though." Then Sidekick's standing tall on his hinds, sniffing the air like a hound dog. "We're close. I can smell the rotted human flesh. Past that ridge. Keep your eyes peeled. The main event is coming."

The way the bastard grins unnerves me. Like he knows all the secrets and enjoys keeping me in the dark. But based on what I'd seen so far and where we were headed, I have a fairly good idea what's coming next.

11

We reach the tree line with sunrise minutes away. The graveyard looms large, carrying on for as long as the eye can see. Tombstones are spread out like a mile-long cornfield, their granite exteriors weathered, tilted, and broken from years of neglect. An eerie crimson haze hovers menacingly like a coating of blood on the sky. I notice a partial paw print on the nearest grave and follow it onto the hallowed ground.

The stench of human remains and decay growing thicker with every step. Despite the morning dew, the rotted grass crackles under my feet, as if it's as dead as everything else here. As we make our way deeper, rows of granite dominate the view, like we're in the middle of a spider's web and the graves are the threads that spiral out in every direction. The sun peeks out behind the mountains to my west, casting an all-encompassing shadow, and it dawns on me that this just might be the one true Valley of Death.

"Fear no evil," I mutter.

"Losing your balls?" asks Sidekick.

I reload and recheck the SD9 and make sure I have easy access to my machete. "Getting ready to protect 'em," I answer. The entire place reeks of evil, like a thick invisible cloud that sends every fiber of my being into overdrive. The hairs on the back of my neck stand out like antennae. "This place must be God's cesspool." My eyes dart about. My nostrils catch a whiff of sulfur in the air.

Sidekick smells it too. He's on his hinds, tippy-toed, sniffing the air like it's a cool summer breeze. He stops, gazes at me hard. "Actually, it's Hell's beach front property," he says with a pointy ear to pointy ear grin. "Get ready. Here they come."

I look around and don't see anything. But that's to be expected. The zombies will be coming from beneath. Yet, despite the fact that I'm ready for 'em, something grabs my ankle before I react. I look down and see rotted flesh hanging from bony fingers that grip me. The zombie's other arm punches through the dirt. It bends at the elbow, and I don't plan on being here when it fully pushes itself free. I hack the wrist until it severs and jump back, prying the dead fingers off me by hand. I'm eye level with the head that emerges. It's worn and gray with a few straggles of tangled blond hair. One of its eyeballs hangs to the side by a sliver of muscle tissue. Part of its forehead is peeled back partially revealing its skull.

I place two rounds in its distorted face. Bone fragments shatter but it still rises. I step around it and place two more where its brain should be. The skull gives. A splash of gray matter oozes out. But still, it comes. This is the third time I've encountered zombies. The first was with gypsies in Bulgaria, the second on the coasts of Norway. Both times was nasty business, but this is the first time a head shot didn't do the trick.

I look at Sidekick. There are three rising behind him and he couldn't care less. He waits until they're fully out of the ground before he acts. He's in an upright offensive stance, coiled with the grace of a true warrior. He steps on a long branch, flips it up, and catches it in his front paw. Then, with lightning reflexes, he spins and jams it through the middle one's neck. Its head flops to the side but it steps towards him anyway. Sidekick dodges a slow, lame swipe and, ironically enough, sidekicks one into the next, toppling all three of them.

"Which way?" he says, practically ordering me to stay on the trail. I tilt my head in the right direction. But before we go, Sidekick withdraws the branch from the zombie's neck then stabs another one of them through the eye with it. He chuckles as he sees that doesn't even halt its movements. The friggin' things just won't die. Worse, more start rising out of the ground. "Let's go," Sidekick says to me, as if none of this bothers him.

I ain't about to argue. I back step away from a zombie's lumbering swipe and shoot it in the knee. It falls, though now it's crawling towards me. "These undead creeps are nothing if not persistent," I say, moving forward. I double the pace of my tracking, putting some distance between us, thankful that the zombies are as slow as snails in a snowstorm. A peek back shows at least a dozen following us.

The ground's getting softer. I spot a series of wolf tracks easy to follow. They lead even deeper into the yard. I'm running full speed. Sidekick's trotting, yet still way ahead of me making me wish I had him on a leash. At least we're putting some distance between us and the undead. I notice the tracks we're following are now headed in both directions, so I know we're close. Then the trail stops dead at one particular grave. There's a hole dug, at least six feet deep. The dirt pile looks fresh. I look at the tombstone and it's surprisingly smooth, like it's brand new. Then I read what's inscribed on it and all my instincts tell me I'm fucked.

R.I.P. Frank Jones is written in all capital letters. *Old Man Jones.* Underneath 1932-2014. In between… Hellraiser.

My mind scrambles to put the jigsaw puzzle together. Most of it immediately clicks, including the fact that Jones wasn't the decent man I thought he was, but I still can't place a few pieces. I'll have to figure those out later. I quickly scout for an exit but zombies are rising around the perimeter faster than weeds in my Aunt Bessie's garden. I turn. Sidekick can't stop laughing. And who could blame 'em. This whole adventure has been one big joke and I'm the punch line. But I'll be damned if I'm dying alone. I fire a shot almost point blank into Sidekick's chest. Unfortunately, it's not silver. He shrugs it off like Superman, smacks the gun from my hand, grabs hold of my hair, and lifts me off the ground like I was a toy. My feet dangle which, as a little person, really pisses me off.

"Why now?" I ask. "Why not kill me at the stable, or back at your den? Why not let little rabbit Fufu take a bite out of me?"

He tilts his head toward the ground and I notice it, an arc of charcoal colored ash. My eyes follow it and I see it surrounds me in a circle with about a twenty yard diameter. Ten yards behind that the zombie hoards stop, forming an inhuman wall. I study the circle and see interlacing lines of ash that form a pentagram, all very skillfully blended in with the dirt and shadow. I've already figured out it's Massan, ash of the dead. I'm familiar with the pentagram too. It supposedly represents the five wounds of Christ, the five points of the human body, or the five elements; earth, fire, water, air, and spirit. However, this one's inverted, meaning it represents black magic and evil… the dark side of eternity and infinity. Simply put, I'm trapped within a circle of Hell.

Sidekick lays out the plan just to show me how stupid I am. "Because in order for the spell to work, the blood sacrifice must enter the circle of their own free will."

And there's one of the missing pieces. For whatever reason, Old Man Jones was the original willing sacrifice. Who knows what he was promised or what would make him do it, but demons have a way of being persuasive.

Sidekick continues. "I never liked you, Silas. But I never figured you were this much of an imbecile. Hell Pack isn't six rebel wolves. Our entire clan is Hell Pack."

He pauses for a second, letting the horrifying implications of that sink into my brain. The treaty was never real. It just kept us away from them until they were ready to strike. He lifts me higher, adding humiliation to my pain to afford me a better view.

"Welcome to the Gate, Silas Hill. Thanks for being the key." His claws lash out, slashing me across the chest. My blood splatters on the tombstone and dribbles on the ground. A gust of wind rises out of nowhere, kicking up the Massan around the perimeter.

"You really pulled out all the stops for me." I spit right in his eye.

He wipes it then I scream as he claws my leg, feeding more of my blood to the ritual. The wind whips up another notch, scattering dirt and debris everywhere. Sidekick momentarily shields his eyes and I try using the opportunity to get free. I struggle like a swamp rat as the ground starts rumbling beneath our feet. He stumbles, which gives me a moment to grab a dagger from my belt. I'd love to stick it in his throat, but I can't reach and it wouldn't have any more effect than the bullet. No silver, no harm. So I reach up and slice the knife through my hair, cutting myself loose. I drop and roll, the ground cracking beneath us. A patch of dirt disappears into the earth as if taken by the suction of a powerful unseen vacuum. A cloud of charcoal smoke puffs back in return. The smell of brimstone and sulfur overtake the smell of the dead. I see the SD9 I dropped then watch it disappear as a second whoosh sucks it into the earth.

"Nowhere to go, Silas. If I don't get to pick your bones clean, the Devil will," says Sidekick, as he steps back to safety.

The Devil. That's too fucked up to even think about. I'm hoping he's full of shit, but somehow I don't think he is. The wind around us starts whipping faster, making it hard to breathe, and all the while, Sidekick's laughing it up like he won the lottery. Fissures form directly along the lines of ash and more dirt crumbles inward. I scramble to my feet and race out of the circle as far away from Sidekick as I can. I try brushing the ash as I cross over the mystic lines, hoping against hope that somehow it disrupts the spell.

It doesn't. The ground within grows hotter as a full sinkhole forms, ripped inward into a fiery black vortex... a perfectly circular chasm, a direct tunnel to death. I'm ready to bolt for the hills, but the zombies block my way, four or five thick in every direction. I'm trapped between a dead human outer wall and the doorway to Hell, stuck in the middle ring with an alpha werewolf who will never let me leave here alive.

The sinkhole breathes fire, like the top of a volcano. Sidekick is looking down from the edge, his arms wide, trying to catch a glimpse of what's to come. I slowly back away so I'm equidistant between the pit and the unmoving zombies. There's nothing I can do but watch, a ringside seat to the beginning of the end of the world.

12

A horrifying sound, louder than the scream of a banshee, emanates from the pit, alerting the world that the Devil's on his way and there's nothing anyone can do to stop it. It overpowers the moans of the zombies. I start to mutter a curse under my breath when I realize there isn't one strong enough to describe just how fucked up this is. Then I hear another sound… the roar of motorcycle engines coming from the distance, growing louder, getting closer.

A moment later, it's pure chaos. To my left, a row of zombies get knocked over like bowling pins as a riderless motorcycle slides across the dirt, plowing through them. Four of the zombies go flying into the fiery pit. The Harley follows, its wheels spinning like buzz saws. It cuts another zombie in half before it too catapults into the pit. A burst of flames shoots up from the abyss as if someone poured too much gasoline on a barbecue.

It's a wakeup call, like a starter's pistol that begins a race. What was potential energy a moment ago is now in motion. The zombies are no longer a wall but an advancing army attacking from every direction. The *ratatatat* of machine gunfire echoes everywhere. The walking dead splatter, colorful crap flying everywhere and suddenly I'm in the middle of a Quentin Tarantino movie. But I don't have time for popcorn. A zombie cluster is coming my way.

I pivot away from a clumsy lunge, my knife already moving in a sweeping motion. The blade goes right through its eye, but the damned thing doesn't stop. Its teeth snap at my hand, its arms reach up to grab mine. I pull my hand back, avoiding it, but it costs me the knife. Once again, I was stupid. I'm acting on zombie killing instinct, one, which in this case, doesn't seem to apply. I have to stop going for the head. It doesn't stop them. I need to limit their mobility.

It lunges at me again. I sidestep, coil my right leg then drive my boot into its kneecap, hearing the satisfying snap. It buckles unable to complete its next lunge. But five more are right behind it. I go for my axe, but two jump me simultaneously, driving me back before I get a firm grip. Saliva drools from their mouths. I roll back, grabbing whatever I can of their tattered cloth. Then, using their own momentum against them, I plant my legs into their stomachs and monkey flip them into the pit. I quickly roll to the side as another attempts to dive on top of me. I avoid it but crash into three more that moved in from my left. Their hands grab me. Mine finally find my axe. I chop off an arm. On the way back, my axe imbeds into one of their kidneys. I don't have time to get it back. Teeth are coming for me. I thrust my palm into the jaw of one bending down to bite me. Out of the corner of my eye, I see another diving at my legs. I pull my right leg into me then thrust it out, my boot caving in the side of its rotted, dried up face.

It was a good shot, but I'm completely overwhelmed. More of them pile forward, forcing me down by their sheer weight. My hands and feet start moving with lightning like quickness that only pure panic can provide. I catch one in the jaw with my knee. One comes for my neck. I push my thumb through its eye socket, lifting its head enough so I can crush its windpipe with an elbow strike. Three quick jabs momentarily push back three more of them. I kick another in its shoulder. Each move buying me another split second of life. One miss, one bit of let up, and it's all over. I figure that'll happen in less than five seconds.

I hear a boom and I'm sprayed with body parts. The nearest zombie collapses on me like a wet sack. I push it forward as a second boom sends one of the zombies holding me down into the pit. The pressure on me subsides and I actually think it's possible now that I could fight my way to my feet.

"Stay down," a strong voice yells out. I listen. Then the *rattatat* of a machine gun goes nuts. Zombies are jerking around me under the onslaught of unrelenting lead. It showers red and gray all over me and I'm not wearing a raincoat. Fragments of bone sting my skin. Something soft and moist hits my mouth. I roll over, so more zombie parts don't hit me in the face.

Finally, it stops. I push what's left of the zombie meat off of me, get to my feet, and wipe a sleeve across my face. Father Miguel's towering above me, white priest collar around his neck, ammunition strapped across his chest. Smoke drifts from the barrel of his machine gun. He looks like Clint Eastwood auditioning for an Exorcist movie. He drops a heavy green sack at my side. It opens and three semi-automatics spill out. I can tell by the way they hit the ground they're all fully loaded.

"Pick one, son. Heck, pick 'em all." He twirls, rapidly turning his machine gun, putting more of the zombie fucks down. Everyone he hits with a burst to the chest drops like a stone. "Aim for their hearts," he says. "These aren't ordinary zombies. They're demon made. Taking out their hearts is the only way to stop them."

More zombies are pushing towards us now like an unruly crowd at Walmart on Black Friday. I pick up one of the guns and run out the magazine before they get the chance to force us backward into the pit. I discharge it and bend down to grab the next one when I catch a flash of black fur moving sideways through the crowd. *Sidekick.* By the time I clutch the weapon in my hand and get my head back up to get a good look where he is, he's gone. I frantically scan the crowd but I'm forced to engage anything coming at me so I can't complete a thorough search. By the time I see him again, it's too late.

He's on Miguel in the space between heartbeats, driving him into the ground. Sidekick's in half-human, half-wolf form. His fingers are spread wide, his shimmering claws ready to slash Miguel wide open. Miguel's weapon gets lost, dropping out of reach and into the pit. I raise mine, but Sidekick sees me and reacts faster than I can get a shot off. He lunges and some part of him that's hard and furry catches the side of my head. I go down. My vision's blurred but I hear and feel Sidekick kick my gun away.

"God, I love punching you in the face," he says, as if God has any place here. "It's all over, Silas. You, humanity, everything. The Devil's on his way and he has two armies to conquer with.

Zombies and werewolves killing and destroying all of mankind. I wanted you to know that before you died."

He hoists me in the air, one hand gripping my throat, the other wrapped around my crotch, an unpleasant amount of pressure on my delicates. I look into the abyss he's about to throw me in… a true hellhole engulfed in hellfire.

"Any final words, Silas?"

"Go to hell," I squeeze out.

"I don't have to. Hell's coming here," he says.

Sidekick arches his arms back and I brace myself for the fall that's coming. But then a single shot rings out and he buckles. Another shot drops him to his knees as I drop off to his side.

"Why don't you pick on someone your own size," my Pa says. His muscles are bulging out of his short sleeve, blood-soaked, khaki t-shirt. His M27 Infantry Automatic Rifle is clutched against his shoulder, his finger leaning on the trigger. He's pissed. I can see the vein bulging from his forehead. No one ever walks away unscathed when the vein comes out.

"I think I will," says Sidekick. He lunges at my pa with lightning speed.

My pa doesn't even flinch. He squeezes the trigger and unleashes every bullet left in his 30 round STANAG magazine. I have the pleasure of watching Sidekick's body convulse under a barrage of silver bullets. He hits the ground like a hairy clump of red and black dog goo with blood spurting from the wounds. My only regret is that the honor of killing him wasn't mine.

I stand up. My pa gets a good look at me and, as tough as he is, I can see the wince on his face. "Shitty night?" he asks.

"You have no idea," I answer. I look at Sidekick again. There's barely enough of his face left to see what species he is. I'm fairly certain my pa didn't miss a single shot. "He so had that coming," I say to Pa.

"Happy to oblige," he answers. "Any need for more silver?" he asks, seeing only a smattering of walking zombies left in the area. The rest of them are lying around like litter in the graveyard.

"Save the silver. We're going to need it later," I say. "If there is a later," I add.

My pa nods. He reloads with a standard clip and takes out a few more zombies on the other side of the pit. He lowers the rifle, puzzled. "They're backing off. Any idea why?"

Miguel's back on his feet now, with us. "Their master has ordered them to," he says.

We all know what it means. Flames shoot skyward from the pit to confirm it. We back away, shielding our eyes from the heat and the bright flash of light. Then the world rumbles once more, the vibration building to an ear-splitting crescendo. A moment later *he* emerges.

I've heard he comes in many forms. For this entrance, he's chosen the most terrifying. His body is a hulking mass of ripped red muscle, nothing at all like the gentlemanly appearance you read about. I estimate his height at around nine-feet tall. His wings arc out angular and long like a prehistoric pterodactyl. His clawed hooves dig into the dirt in front of us, as if he owns the earth. His hands are massive, his fingers threateningly bend, properly displaying his razor-sharp talons. His face is that of a goat, but with predatory fangs and thick, slightly curled, elongated horns. His odor is foul and repulsive. He is, by far, the scariest motherfucker I have ever seen, and I've seen some of the scariest.

The three of us instinctively step back. Father Miguel crosses himself and the devil laughs.

"Hello, Father Miguel Santos, Jebediah Hill. How nice to greet you… *again*." His eyes slant and a puff of smoke comes out of his nose. Then his gaze turns to me and I swear his black eyes can see my soul. "Have you brought me your other son to kill?"

I swallow, the overwhelming fear mixing with the knowledge that the Devil himself is my brother's killer.

Father Miguel steps forward. "Your foul presence has no place in this realm of the living. Your summoning was involuntary and thus not in accordance with celestial rules. Be gone, now, lest the forces of Heaven itself rise up against you," he screams.

The Devil leans in. The smoke coming from his goat nostrils cover Miguel's face. "Blow smoke up someone else's ass, Father. From this day forth, your world is mine." He flaps his wings, hovering a few feet in the air. "Rise," he commands, spreading his powerful arms wide.

He's looking at us, laughing, reveling in our fear and despair. With his gesture, more corpses awaken from their dirtnap and push up from below. I try to take a quick count of all the distorted, hideous, rotted ghouls, but there are far too many of them. An army of hundreds of zombies are rising from the graves.

13

Werewolves, zombies, and the Devil.

This is the triple fuck of all fucks and if me, my pa, and Father Miguel can't stop 'em, the human race is doomed. Yet, what we're supposed to do against this I have no idea. I remember I'm still holding an M27 semi-automatic and decide to use it. I fire as many shots as my trigger-happy finger can get off right into the Devil's chest. The bullets bounce off as if his skin was made of armor.

He swoops down and grabs me in his big fist like I'm a doll. My pa makes an effort to hold onto me, but the Devil effortlessly nudges him away and takes me with him into the air. I don't catch my breath until he stops around a few hundred feet high. His grip is so powerful, his fist so large, I don't even have room to struggle. He smiles at me and licks his lips like I'm a snack.

"You must be Silas. Still *little* after all these years," he mocks.

"You killed my brother, asshole," I say.

"He was the price your father paid me for your mother," the Devil responds to me. I don't understand. He sees the look on my face and knows he's found a weak spot. "Oh, I see. Your father never told you how we met."

I'm not sure I even want to know what he's talking about. "Go fuck yourself," I answer.

He's unfazed. "You should thank me. I could have chosen you," he says back. He holds me out, away from his body, his dark eyes scanning me. I can tell he doesn't like what he sees. "Hmmm… perhaps my initial assessment was wrong." He dives down, descending like a bird of prey, and there's not much I can do about it but helplessly go along for the ride. He stops short, a foot off the ground, and deposits me at my father's feet like a stork delivering a baby.

"Are you done?" I scowl at him.

He smiles then looks at my pa and snorts. "Your son has a pure soul. Looks like the two of you need to have a father son talk. Perhaps that will color it a bit." Then the Devil looks back, admiring his advancing army of zombies. "You better hurry, though. You don't have much time." Then he takes off, literally like a bat out of hell.

"He's heading to Los Agros," says Miguel. "We need to go, now," he adds, raising his gun, firing a few bursts of scattershot that drop the two zombies closest to us. One of 'em rises back up. Miguel aims more carefully and finishes him off for good.

My father grabs my arm and lifts me up. Our eyes meet. I see the shame in his. He knows the Devil just revealed to me his darkest secret. Now I know the Devil spoke true.

"I—" Pa starts to explain, but Miguel cuts him off.

"Not now… Balzuzu's right. We don't have much time," says Miguel. He tilts his head at the advancing hoard of corpses. Their sickening moans fill the air with despair. Their stench washes over us like a gray cloud. "Nor do we have enough ammo to deal with them. Our only hope lies in Los Agros."

Pa looks at me, almost apologetically.

"I agree," I say loudly. Then I turn to my pa, soften my tone and add, "anything you have to tell me can wait until later… if there is a later."

Pa nods and it's time to move. We backpedal toward a motorcycle lying on its side. Miguel fires indiscriminately at anything non-living that approaches. "Who's Balzuzu?" I ask him. "I thought that was the Devil."

"Balzuzu is a devil. He's not *the* Devil," Father Miguel answers. "He's Nephilim… a descendant of Araqiel, a savage that resides in the space between Heaven and Earth."

Miguel's words are just as confusing as Balzuzu's, but I got the gist. "Since you know who he is, how do we stop him?" I ask, while blasting an approaching zombie into tomato paste.

"We need to get him back on his side of the gate. I know how to perform the ritual that closes it," says Miguel.

"Simple enough… how do we get him there? How do we drive him back?"

"Through the only thing he understands… brute force," answers Miguel.

"Okay… brilliant," I say, a pained smile on my face. In my head I say we're fucked more than a new kid in a prison block.

My pa grabs the motorcycle by the handle and hoists it upright. He steps on the clutch, twists the handle, and the engine roars. The rear wheel kicks up dirt and in a second my pa's next to us. "Get on," he says.

It's built for two. Miguel hops on behind my pa. The zombie herd is closing in. I squeeze in behind Miguel making the bike big enough to fit two and a half.

My pa throttles it. Then he screams out. "Sheriff Martaan got your Wyatt Earp message. The whole town is prepared. But they're prepared for a werewolf invasion, not zombies, and definitely not Balzuzu. We have to get back and warn them."

"It'll be too late. Balzuzu's probably there already," shouts Miguel.

I look back. The few seconds we've logged on the bike have already put a sizable distance between us and the undead. I have an idea. It's a bad one but… "Pa," I scream. "Drop me off at the tree line. I have a stopover to make."

My father alters course, swerving through the tombstones. A dead hand rises up from underneath and attempts to grab the front wheel. We ride over it grinding it to mush. A few moments later, we're where I need to be.

I hop off. "How much silver you got left?" I ask them.

"Six clips. Thirty each," Pa answers. He's already figured out I'm going back for the werewolves. "It's suicide," he adds.

"It's slim to none, but it's our only slim to none," I respond.

"Then I'm going with you," my pa replies.

"No," I insist. "Balzuzu the devil creature… he's the biggest threat. You need to get to our weapons cache, take out everything we've got, and make him eat it."

"This is an unwise course of action. Are you sure, son?" asks Miguel.

"Dead sure," I blurt out with a shrug. It has to be the worst timed joke ever.

My father tosses his satchel at me. I pull out the custom-made wolf killer magazines, lock one of them into place. My pa's staring at me, still deciding if letting me go on my own is the right move. I nod. "You do what you have to do. I've got this," I insist again. He gets the message. We're the Hill family. Come hell or high water—and in this case Hell is here—we do what we have to and take care of business.

"Semper Fi," he says back to me with a salute. He looks ahead, twists the throttle and never looks back.

I race into the forest, quickly finding the trail Sidekick and I used to make our way out here. This time Silver Joe and I will meet on my terms.

14

I zip between the trees, my eyes on constant alert for were-zombie rabbits, supernatural snakes and whatever other paranormal fucked up forest creature inhabit these woods. My thoughts move to Sidekick. Seeing his face turned into pudding by a barrage of silver caps warmed my heart, but the things he talked about chilled my bones; *"Our entire clan is Hell Pack,"* *"Because in order for the spell to work, the blood sacrifice must enter the circle of their own free will,"* *"Zombies and werewolves killing and destroying all mankind."*

So, if the werewolves were in on it the whole time and Old Man Jones was their blood sacrifice then why did the werewolves kill Old Man Jones before he got to the graveyard? Then I remember… the werewolves didn't kill him. *A* werewolf killed him. A rogue werewolf that Silver Joe said was an outsider to their pack. A werewolf that I put down for good because I assumed he was the problem.

It's still not making sense to me. A snake slithers across my path. I can't tell if it's of the supernatural variety so I run around it instead of wasting the bullets. I glance back and see it doesn't follow. But the trees behind it are familiar. I make the mental note that soon I'll be crossing back into werewolf territory.

I take the inconsistency of Old Man Jones' murder puzzle and flip it around in my head so I can see it from a different angle. The actions of the lone werewolf couldn't have been a coincidence. It had to have known exactly what it was doing. It had to have known Old Man Jones was the willing sacrifice. That meant he wanted to stop him. He killed Jones to make sure he never made it to the graveyard. *So he was working against his own kind.* The question was why? He was an outsider. Maybe he just wanted to piss them off.

But then why did he lay Jones out like that? I'm reminded of what he said to me before I put a bullet through his skull by the lakefront. *"Just sending a message. The old man made a good piece of paper."* I asked him from who. I think the question I should have asked was *for* who, because if he, and the entire werewolf population knew, then that message had to be for us… or more specifically *for me, my pa, or Miguel.* We were the only three who knew exactly how my brother was killed. But it was clear the lone werewolf also knew.

My leg feels wet. It's my blood. My adrenalines been pumping so fast I forgot about the wounds Sidekick inflicted on me. I'm well into his territory now. My gun's at the ready for when any of them get in my way. But something feels off; the forest around me is quiet... *too quiet.* That means every werewolf that lives here is either at the den preparing for the attack order or they're already in town with Balzuzu. I'm already too committed to my course of action. I can only hope it's the former and I'm not too late to stop them. I quicken my pace as best I can.

My mind goes back to my working theory and it dawns on me. Lone Wolf was leaving us a warning. He killed Jones to prevent the devil's ascension into this world then laid out the body so we'd investigate and learn the truth. Jones *was* a lure... but not to lure me into a trap, to trick me into discovering the truth. And when Silver Joe and Sidekick found out what Lone Wolf did, they sent a kill squad to eliminate him. But the six of them, Scout and his crew, found me instead. It's starting to make sense to me now and I'm more the fool for understanding. It was brilliant stratagem. Lone Wolf got me to see the real threat and Silver Joe was smart enough to turn the situation around by making me the new sacrifice. The solution fills me with clarity, a newfound sense of purpose to correct my mistakes.

I hear a cacophony of howls reverberate through the morning sky, a prelude to the coming bloodshed highlighted with the cadence of a battle cry for a war I thought I averted. I'm thankful for it. It means they're still here and their hollers cover up my footfalls.

I sneak close, finding a spot on higher ground that affords me a clear view of their den. They're all there; a hundred of them, maybe more. They're lined up, ready to march. The ones near the front are on their hinds, fully upright. The ones in formation are all wolf. They're all so busy hooting and howling, not a single one of them senses my approach. Silver Joe is in front. I find a perfect hiding spot to spy on them just as he raises a paw to quiet them down. I could blow his head off from here. End his life right now then kill as many of these bastards on their home turf before they have the chance to get to ours.

Instead, I listen.

"The time has come. Today is the day we do what we were created to do," says Silver Joe. A few wolves bark their approval. Joe settles them down. The word *created* settles in my head. If I didn't know better, I would think he's just talking about killing, but Sidekick scoffed when I mentioned he was bitten. He said I didn't know a thing about werewolves. So if people didn't become werewolves because they were bitten by one then someone had to *create* them to make them the way they were.

Silver Joe continued. "The devil has come to Los Agros…"

Or *something!*

"…The devil has come to this world."

Balzuzu! Balzuzu made them…

"It's time to do what the devil born us to do," yells Silver Joe to the howls of his pack.

Fuck this! I run out from my hiding spot, my M27 cocked and ready. I step into the den of wolves, halt at the perimeter, the semi-automatic pointed directly at Silver Joe. In a second, all feral eyes are on me. Joe sees he no longer has their attention, turns to see why, and sees me. Surprise registers on his face. Then primal anger takes its place.

A werewolf moves forward, preparing to attack. I redirect the rifle at him and he pauses. Joe starts forward then I train the rifle back on him and he stops. "All my ammunition is silver," I shout. "Which one of you bastards wants to make me prove it first?" I can see the gears turning in Joe's brain. He's thinking *all* of them. They're all thinking all of them.

"There are two ways this goes down," I shout. "We can slaughter each other to pieces right here, right now. Or… you can join me."

Silver Joe looks baffled. But only for a split second… then he's all leader again. "Join you for what?" he asks with a snarl.

"Quite frankly," I say. "You never struck me as the type to be anyone's bitch."

15

"I know the devil who created you," I shout out to the lot of them. "Only he's not the real devil at all. His name is Balzuzu. He's a *lesser* demon who likes to make himself appear more powerful than he actually is. Silver Joe's snarling, but I can see his entire demeanor has changed. I'm guessing the words *lesser* and *bitch* hit him right between his oversized alpha eyes. I push it. "You go out there and do Balzuzu's bidding… that doesn't end your service to him. It begins it. You want to truly do what you were born to do. You were born *free*."

Two werewolves try to break through the lines to attack me. I could shoot 'em, but I don't have to. Silver Joe grabs one by the scruff of its neck and commands the other one to get back.

"See that, Joe," I prod. "They're already listening to *Balzuzu* instead of you." I make sure I say Balzuzu instead of the devil to take the stigma away.

Joe approaches, slowly, unthreatening. "The devil made us," he insists.

I keep my gun pointed at him, holding onto my position of strength. "Balzuzu made you. That doesn't mean he owns you. You aren't his *pets*," I throw in, another zinger to help change their minds. "I can't see you…" I look to the entire pack and raise my voice "…I can't picture any of you living as his slaves."

There's a long pause. Silver Joe paces back and forth, looking into the eyes of his clan to gain a sense of their take on my words. I try to do the same, but I can't get a feel for them.

One of the wolves comes forward, a large black one with eyes of stone. He's almost as intimidating and powerful looking as Silver Joe. I believe he was the one that carried Scout's body back to the fold. "Balzuzu…" he snorts, mulling over the name. "Balzuzu may be a *lesser* devil, but he's still a powerful one. What's your plan?" he asks, the words dripping from his tongue like saliva.

"Balzuzu's raised an army of zombies. They're heading into town to rip us to shreds. I say we get there and rip them to shreds first."

"And what of Balzuzu?" he asks.

I narrow my angry eyes. "You leave that big red fuck to me."

The black one and I lock eyes. He knows I killed seven of his kind by my lonesome just last night, an act he views not with resentment, but with respect. Now he wants to take my measure for himself. I make sure I give him everything he's looking for.

Silver Joe says, "You're asking us to fight *for* you."

"We're going to war either way. The only question you have is, which side do you want to be on?" I respond.

The black one approaches me again. "The winning side," he snarls.

"Do you really think we're going to let him win?" I ask. "Even if he takes over Los Agros today, do you really think we're going to let that stand tomorrow? That's when our military gets called in; battalions of trained men, attack helicopters, fighter jets, missiles. We have nukes for…" That's when it dawns on me. My voice becomes a whisper. "…god's sake. Hell on earth."

All of a sudden I'm Sherlock fuckin' Holmes and Balzuzu's master scheme unravels itself before me. My expression changes from awe to shock and they notice.

"*Hell on earth…* that's what he wants," I continue, stunned at the thought of it. The big picture scrolls through my head like a horror movie. I see it. It starts in my hometown then spreads out across the globe like an epidemic. Each battle escalates into a larger one, each one the consequences more terrifying, more deadly, the stakes and the body count continually raised until utter annihilation is the only possible outcome. Death and destruction on an unimaginable scale. The fall of mankind… and if it's followed by a long season of nuclear winter so much the better. Balzuzu's victory… not ruling the world, but ruining it. Judgment day. He might as well be the real devil. "Hell on earth," I shout louder. "And you're his pawns. He asks you to kill for him, but what will be left for you?"

A moment passes. A moment they take to think about it. It makes too much sense for them not to.

"Nothing," says Silver Joe.

"That's right… nothing. A barren wasteland empty of anything to hunt. You'll exist without any purpose, except to serve him," I say.

The black one steps toward me. "And if we *do* fight with you, what will you ask of us?"

I lower my weapon. "I could use a ride."

16

"You're a feisty little bastard, ain't ya," the black werewolf says.

He's halfway between upright and wolf, running through the forest gorilla style and I'm holding onto his neck for dear life. The ride's bumpy as heck but I manage. There's no way I'm allowing myself to fall off and look ridiculous, especially since we're smack dab in the middle of the pack, one hundred plus strong, stampeding like a wild herd of buffalo. I look to my right. A brown wolf races by us on all fours. To my left, a gray one is keeping pace, grinning at me like the Cheshire Cat. I can't tell if he's laughing at me or glad to be with me fighting on the right side. I just grin back giving him the best crooked smile I can muster.

"I think he's hoping I drop you so he can grab a bite," says the black one.

I whisper back into my carrier's ear. "You know what they say… the littler they are, the harder they are to make fall."

He chuckles. "I was like you once," he says. "A little person. Cept I didn't have your brass. I allowed myself to be bullied into doing bad things by the wrong folk, which eventually got my ass into all kinds of trouble. Guess that's why I ended up in Hell. Now, I'm big. Nobody fucks with me."

"Balzuzu probably made you like that so you'd be more appreciative," I say.

"Yup! 'Cept now I see he's just another asshole who's bigger than me thinking he can pull my strings."

I'm beginning to like this werewolf. In my head I call him Rebel. He quickens his pace, making it tougher for me to hold on. I grab a chunk of his fur in my fist and lean myself closer into his back. In the distance we hear the sound of gunfire. A lot of it. The war's started without us. There's no break in the staccato of gunfire we hear, the pattern of which smacks of fear and desperation. We pass the tree line into the open field and now I hear screams, too. And not the kind that's excited to fight back, but yells of horror crying out for salvation.

Before we left I told Silver Joe that the zombie's hearts were their weak spots. That that's how you take them down. He gave me another cell and told me to phone ahead to Maartan so that his pack doesn't get taken down as well. Last time I spoke to

Maartan I used the Wyatt Earp code word. That meant no immediate danger but to get prepared in case that changed. This time I called him to tell him to hold onto the silver bullets. No werewolf was to be fired upon unless it attacked first. I sincerely hoped he listened and that Silver Joe wasn't planning on double-crossing me again because we were that salvation. If anything went wrong, if any one from either side didn't act accordingly, the screams were going to get a lot worse.

I tighten my grip, pull myself closer to Rebel, and ask, "What's your top speed?"

He grins, says, "Hang on," and accelerates. We dart through the pack, the others now increasing their pace to keep up with us. We near the front lines and I see it all... all the unspeakable death and madness happening right before my eyes. Zombies are swarming Los Agros like bees after someone poked the hive. They're attacking everything in their path. They're everywhere, coming in continuous waves like rats following the Pied Piper, feeding on the fallen like cockroaches on year-old salami.

The townsfolk, people I once called my neighbors, are spread thin running through the streets, shooting at the walking dead with any gun they have in their arsenal. But they are completely overwhelmed. I recognize Mrs. Garrity, the owner of the town bakery, as she unloads a shotgun blast into a zombie. It crumbles. She cocks the weapon about to fire again, but three zombies tackle her from the side and start ripping her to pieces. Mr. Garrity steps forward with an ax, hacking at them in a desperate attempt to save her. Two zombies grab him from behind and chew into his neck.

Three of Martaan's men, all uniformed, take cover behind a car, aiming purposely and expertly in different directions. Their bullets plug into the corpses approaching them. But their aim isn't true enough. They're too panicked to hit the hearts, so all they're doing is chipping away flesh, bone, and muscle tissue while the decomposed bodies still come for them. They try to flee before they get overrun, but a hoard blocks them in from behind cutting off their retreat.

Preacher Larry runs into the middle of the street, a stern presence, a force to be reckoned with. His first shotgun blast blows a zombie to smithereens. Its guts spray the concrete crimson red. A second blast splatters another. He's yelling to Martaan's men as he reloads. I can't hear what he's saying but he's pointing at his heart, rallying them, telling them where to concentrate their aim. They group together tightly and turn a row of the undead into a row of the Swiss cheese.

Then Balzuzu, the architect of this terrifying insanity, swoops down out of nowhere. Preacher Larry shoots him, but the devil doesn't even flinch as the buckshot ricochets of his thick hide. He grabs Larry with both hands, elevates high enough for everyone to see, and literally rips Larry in half as a display of what will happen to anyone who defies him. Larry's intestines drop from his torso and splash onto the street. Two officers run away, right into a hoard of zombies that start tearing into their flesh. Another officer stands his ground and starts shooting at Balzuzu who simply swoops down again and guts the officer like a fish.

I've fought monsters for years. I've seen gruesome deaths firsthand. Not once have I ever seen carnage like this.

Balzuzu sees us race forth from the forest. It's too bad he hasn't noticed me riding atop Rebel. Too bad for him. He hears our howls and battle cries. His expression tells me he thinks total victory, total annihilation of the people of Los Agros, is at hand. He thinks he's about to witness more slaughter, more needless death that he can relish in. He's right, but he's wrong. It's not the townsfolk that are going to be slaughtered by werewolves. It's his army of zombies.

We come in hard and fast, without an ounce of hesitation in our stride, arriving like the light brigade filled with teeth and claws. Fangs bite down, easily tearing through flesh. Razor-sharp nails slice through organs. But Hell Pack is only ripping into the dead, not the living.

In mid-stride, Rebel bites the head off a zombie about to attack a lost child then glides to a stop to let me off. "Stay safe, my friend," he says.

"You too, friend," I respond. I jump off his back, roll in a somersault, and come up with guns blazing. I double tap the stumbling corpse closest to me. It drops easily and I do the same to the one right behind him. Two z's grab my left shoulder. I back step, reach for the sharpened weapon on my waist, and thrust the machete through one of their hearts. Then I kick the dead zombie into the other one, turn my gun on them and blow them away. I quickly pivot to my right and kill another.

All around me, werewolves are doing the same. I see a dead head roll by. I backtrack its path and see Silver Joe's got a firm grip on its still moving body. He wipes blood from his mouth and snout, discards the headless body into an advancing zombie and savagely goes to work on a few more with his claws. I take out two more with my machete before I spot Rebel. He thrusts his arm through the living corpse in front of him. A second later, he pulls out its decrepit heart which is still beating in his hands.

He sees me, smiles, crushes the squishy red muscle in his large hairy fist, and kills some more. Behind him, a brown werewolf gets bitten by a zombie that jumped on his back. The wolf howls, turns, and gets savage. It's a vicious display of wetwork I didn't need to see.

Everywhere I look it's pure chaos. Nature, or I should say 'unnature', at its most simple, brutal core. There is no mercy, no civilized behavior. It's strictly an unrelenting violent battle where only the strongest and most aggressive will survive. But it's all the sideshow. Balzuzu is the main attraction, the one we need to kill most. Though, with our weapons so far unable to penetrate his armored skin, how we're going to accomplish that is beyond me.

I finally spot the devil and it ain't pretty. He's been betrayed. The look on his face is priceless but someone, probably every one of us, is going to pay. A small pack has him surrounded. A white werewolf lunges forward, its teeth bared going for Balzuzu's throat. Balzuzu catches his head in his big hands, mid-leap, and snaps his neck like it was a twig. The werewolf looks like its head was put on backwards as the devil drops him, readying himself to dish out more punishment. While I'm pondering if a werewolf can heal from an injury like that, two more werewolves jump on Balzuzu's back, sinking their teeth into his wings. Balzuzu rolls forward, tucking his wings in, then he arcs them forward bringing both wolves within reach of his massive hands. He grabs one and throws him at another werewolf about to attack, taking out both with one move. Then he grabs the other werewolf in both hands and rips him in two the same way he did Preacher Larry.

I slash forward with the machete, using it and my guns to plow myself a path through the zombies. I start to race toward Balzuzu, my machete raised. All I'm thinking is that one of those hands has to go. Someone human grabs my shoulder and holds me back.

"You're confusing bravery with stupidity," Pa says. "That's the quickest path to death I've ever seen. We need to hit him with something bigger and harder than he is."

I look around. My eyes catch a black SUV. "I could hot wire that," I say. I think quickly. "Do we have any C-4 at the house? We could rig it to explode. I could drive it right up his a—"

"Plenty, but…" my pa hands me a Heckler & Koch MP5. It's hefty in my grip but I can handle it. "Take this. Take these too," he says handing me extra clips. "Fully automatic and the ammo is explosive incendiary filled with four grams of bullseye powder at the tips. They still may not get through his thick hide, but they should get his attention. Lure him to the church. Backroom. Miguel's sanctuary."

Five zombies attack from the side. I kick one back and test the weapon. The torso I aim at disintegrates in a puff of smoke. Two more splatter that were standing directly behind it. The gun packs a punch. I'll need it too. Bony fingers grab me from my blindside, twisting me, knocking me down. I fire upward feeling the heat as the bullets scorch through its chest. Two are on my pa. I can't risk using the MP5 when they're so close, so I take out my machete and shish kabob one of their hearts. My pa outwrestles the other. In a moment, he's on top of it, his knee on its back. He clasps his hands under its chin and yanks its skull clean off. Its body is squirrelling on the ground like a beheaded chicken. I stick my machete through its back and it stops.

My pa hands me a thin metal strip about the length of my hand. "Even more important, if at all possible, attach this to his back. The ends are coated with a powerful adhesive." My pa shows me a strip of his own. "I have one too. Only one of us has to be successful."

"Looks like an aluminum Band-Aid. What is it?" I ask.

"Miguel refers to it as a higher calling," Pa smirks. "It's—" something catches his attention and he glances up.

It's Balzuzu and he's heading straight for us.

17

The devil's charging like a bull, swatting aside zombie and werewolf and anything else that's in his way as he makes a straight line for us. He steps on a zombie, squishing it beneath his hooves. A wolf comes at him from the side and he smacks it away as easily as if it's a gnat.

My pa pivots, his weapon raised at Balzuzu. An instant later his fully automated submachine gun is firing round after round that hits Big Red square in his barrel chest, the bullets exploding on impact with a violent burst of heat and smoke. A volley like that would have killed any other monster. In Balzuzu's case, it merely slows him down.

He lets loose a frightening roar before beginning with the threats. "You will regret that you have annoyed me. I will skin you alive then rip the meat from your bones. I—"

My pa adjusts his aim so his next volley goes right into Balzuzu's ugly goat mouth. It shuts him up. He stops running then spits out a spent cartridge in an exhale of black smoke.

"Your soul is mine. That is a promise," Balzuzu screams.

My pa continues firing. Balzuzu tilts his head down while bringing his massive arms up to shield his face, blocking the barrage of oncoming bullets, slowly continuing his approach. I raise my H & K and fire a burst of ammo into his thick gut. The bullets make a pinging sound as they bounce off him, but by the way he's howling I can tell they're stinging him even if they aren't penetrating his thick skin.

Pa quickly refits another clip. This ammo's different… a relentless spray of gunfire that shoots faster but doesn't explode upon impact. The bullets hit Balzuzu but ricochet off in every direction, destroying whoever or whatever is around him. My pa keeps up the pressure, unleashing the full clip in an up and down motion, while I'm aiming everywhere he's not so we're hitting Balzuzu everywhere at once. Three werewolves seize our advantage and attack him from the sides. Balzuzu knocks one away, which allows me to fire a burst into his face that irks him enough where he shrieks and takes off into the skies.

"Now he's really pissed," I say, watching him arc around back in our direction.

"We got his attention," says Pa. "The church is two blocks away. Let's go."

The street we run down is a chock full of zombies. We fire enough bullets to make dead beef stew. My pa yells, "Run." I start to, but he doesn't come with me. Balzuzu's already back, bearing down on him and my pa wants to give me a bigger head start. I see him firing everything he's got as Balzuzu swoops in for the kill. But this time the red devil isn't stopped. He knocks the gun out of Pa's hands then grabs him by the waist. My pa fights to get free but Balzuzu head butts him in the face with his horns.

An unsettling smile crosses Balzuzu's twisted face. I turn, raise my gun to fire, but Balzuzu holds my pa between us, using him as a shield, practically daring me to take the shot. I don't, knowing wherever I aim, Balzuzu will simply move my pa into the path of the bullet. He would love to taint my soul by having me be the one that kills my father.

"You're not as dumb as you look, Silas," he yells. Then he looks at my pa, "I will kill you, Jebediah. But first I'm going to eviscerate your other son while you watch." He slams Pa into the ground hard enough where I know he ain't getting up then he's glares at me the way a cat glares at a mouse.

I'm as likely to survive this as a hen in a fox house and both of us know it. I don't even bother to fire. I turn on a dime and sprint toward the church like the north wind. I can feel the vibrations behind me as Balzuzu stomps forward, his hooves cracking the concrete street as he chases me. In the open street I'm too easy to pick off. So, in desperation, I do the most insane thing possible. I dart to my left, and at the last possible moment before Balzuzu can grab me, I dive into a horde of zombies.

There are dozens of them. The stench of their decay is sickening, the touch of their rotted flesh grotesque. They threaten to smother me in death, but before they can pile on me, I'm on my back with my gun obliterating everything inhuman around me. I'm making a big mess of body parts, splattering blood and guts everywhere thinking maybe Balzuzu will lose me in all the confusion. There's a pickup truck a few feet away. I push off my legs, scoot on my back, as I continue firing, bringing me closer to it. Then I roll beneath it to temporary safety, hoping I've either given Balzuzu the slip or he'll think the zombies got to me first and cheated him of the kill he wanted.

The other side of the truck is clear. I roll out and bolt down the street, sprinting about fifty yards before the big fuck reacquires me in the chaos. Our eyes meet. He sees the fear in mine. He's laughing now, strangely satisfied by my resilience, knowing he has me once again.

I'm just one block away from the church. It may as well as be a mile. The street is littered with overturned cars, unmoving corpses, and the newly dead. As I quicken my run, Balzuzu starts coming. He's not running this time. He's flying fast, no longer fucking around. He wants me and he wants me bad. He's close enough to snatch me when my two new best friends make their play. Silver Joe and Rebel pounce on him from behind. They've seen what he can do, so their attack is more cautious, more measured, but no less vicious. Silver Joe goes high for one of the wings. Rebel goes low biting an ankle.

Balzuzu gets his long fingers on Joe's fur, so Rebel bounces up and slashes him across the face, causing him to release Joe. When Joe drops he goes for the same ankle Rebel tried working on. Their movements are coordinated and strategic, their plan to hobble him in some way, limit his mobility. First wound then go for the kill. It's a good strategy, but even with their superhuman strength they can't break the demon's skin. Balzuzu's too strong.

And too fast.

His hooves catch Joe in the underbelly. His sharp fingernails slash down and rip through Silver Joe's side. But Joe is one tough lobo. He takes it, twists inward, and sinks his teeth into Balzuzu's arm, giving Rebel the opening he needs to go for the throat.

Rebel's teeth bite down hard around the demon's neck. Balzuzu brings his elbow down cracking Rebel's back. Silver Joe springs up and grabs Balzuzu's lower jaw, trying his best to snap it off. It's as savage a fight as I've ever seen, but to stay here and watch does my new friends a disservice. They've given me an opportunity. I need to make the most of it.

I take a knee and get the gun's barrel tucked into my shoulder. I'm only going to get one shot at this so I better make it count. I get Big Red's head lined up in my scope. Despite the brawl he's in, he has the look of someone totally in control. And who could blame him. So far we've hit him with everything we have and there's not even a single scratch on his surface. There's blood on him, but not a single drop is his. I focus the laser sight on his right eye hoping to change that. His skin may be as tough as a tank, but I doubt his eyeball lens has the same impenetrable density. Perhaps one well-placed bullet could end it all. But it's the longest of long shots and the way they're thrashing about, I can't get a solid bead on it.

Instead I come up with a better idea... something that will really piss him off and put all of his attention back on me. I raise the gun slightly higher then fire a three-round burst at the top of his head. Two of the bullets hit their mark, his left curly horn, putting a crack in it. My next shot breaks it clean off as the bullet explodes off the top of his head. I log it in my file of all-time favorite monster moments.

He roars with anger, searching for me, knowing full well where the shot came from. I yell out to make it easy for him. "Hey, Clifford. Over here, asshole."

His anger looks legendary. Rebel goes for his head and gets backfisted down the block. Silver Joe gets it even worse… claws through his rib cage followed by a hand that crushes them to powder. Balzuzu's hurt them, but he's no longer interested in their deaths. He's only interested in mine. He darts toward me, an enormous bird of prey on a low altitude trajectory. Time for part two of my wiseass idea. There's an overturned car in his path. I shoot a burst into the gas tank and when the incendiary ammo makes contact with the fuel line its great balls of fire. The flame engulfs him, which he's probably used to, but the shockwave showers him with sharp debris and hurls him down the street.

He's staggered, on his knees. Black blood trickles down his face. A sharp piece of metal protrudes from his leg. First I took his horn. Now, I actually cut the fucker. I'm immensely pleased. I've wanted to stick something in this son of a bitch since the moment he emerged from the pit. Now I had one more thing to stick him with or, more accurately, stick to him. My pa said attaching this strip of metal to him was important. Now seems like the best time as I'm probably not going to get a better chance.

It's my turn now to charge Balzuzu. He's still low to the ground, shaking off the effects of the blast. I run in an arc, so my approach is from behind. While he's yanking the shrapnel from his leg, I leap on his back, attach the adhesive metal strip in midstride, then plant my palm on his shoulder and propel myself over him in a neatly tucked somersault. When I hit the ground, I turn it into a shoulder roll and fire a bullet that ricochets off his forehead in a ping of smoke. I'd love to empty the clip but I can't spare the time. I have a date with God. It's time for me to get the fuck out of here.

I race to the church as Balzuzu lets out a bellow that's loud enough to rip open the sky. Except it's not the sky he wants to rip open. It's me. The church doors are a sprint away. I figure ten seconds to get there, three more to pry them open and get inside. I hear Balzuzu running after me. His footfalls are thunderous. The street vibrates with every step he takes.

Seven seconds. Either I make it to the doors in time or I'm going to die.

18

I turn my head for a microsecond and see Balzuzu's closer than I thought. A part of my brain is telling my body to shit itself, which would be a problem because that would really slow me down. But even without the extra weight in my shorts, I know I'm not going to make it.

So fuck the door. While still running full speed, I shoot out the stained-glass window at ground level, circling my shots to make the opening as wide as possible. I feel the rush of air behind me. Balzuzu is right there, swiping at me, narrowly missing as I dive through the window. The glass I didn't blast away shatters as I crash through it. A few shards cut my skin. I hit the marble church floor shoulder first then keep rolling until my momentum smacks me against a pew.

The thick bricks that encase the window concave inward as Balzuzu's giant body collides with it. But the stone is centuries old and holds. Balzuzu sticks his head through the window and glares at me with a look that could kill a ghost. "I'm going to turn your body inside out and devour your soul," he says. The scary part is he truly fucking means it.

His head disappears. An instant later he collides with the wall again, hard enough to shake the bedrock. A few bricks buckle, landing and cracking as they hit the floor. The remainder of the wall still holds. Though a few more hits like that one and he'll be through, and I'm fuck sure not hanging around here like it's a waiting room. I get to my feet and haul ass down the aisle. There's a door on the right side of the altar that leads to Father Miguel's sanctum sanctorum. That's where I need to go. I'm halfway there when the wall gives in and Balzuzu's inside, a cloud of debris shrouding his entrance.

"Better pray," he hollers.

I turn just enough to give him the finger and keep on running.

His anger's getting the better of him now. He's coming after me, but taking the time to smash the pews into little wooden pieces as he runs through them, a fearsome display of strength that gives me the extra seconds I need to reach the door. I twist the knob and dart through the narrow doorframe, slamming the door shut behind me as if that's going to stop him. I baseball slide down the flight of steps in front of me just as Balzuzu reduces the door and the frame around it to rubble. Oak splinters fly over my head, a reminder to me that if I stop running he'll do the same to my bones.

Miguel's room is through the open archway a few yards down the hall. I make a bee line as Balzuzu roars and pounds the walls causing web-like cracking patterns every time his fist smashes the marble. He can't maneuver as easily in the confined space. This particular hallway wasn't designed to accommodate hulking nine-foot tall giants from Hell. It slows him down enough, letting me get into the large chamber with a big lead.

It's the same huge empty white room I remember being in years ago when Miguel examined my brother's body. But there is one notable exception. A canvas sheet is covering something rather large off on the far right side. Father Miguel's standing next to it, fists closed, staring at me, waiting for the devil to come in.

I don't like the setup. Balzuzu's going to be happy in here. The ceiling rises a hundred feet high and the area is wide enough where Balzuzu could maneuver easily and fly free. Worse, there isn't a single place for us to run or hide, save for a door leading outside which we would never reach in time. We were trapped.

I ran next to Father Miguel, fear in my eyes. He showed none. He simply nodded and raised a finger, a gesture displaying conviction and control.

"Have faith," he told me.

The foundation shakes as Balzuzu's thunders into the room, his massive powerful fists redesigning and widening the archway. His fingernails dig into the hardened marble walls. I momentarily imagine them digging into our significantly softer bodies. I could tell by the smirk on Balzuzu's goat face that he's probably imagining it as well, visualizing it in all its gory details. I see him quickly scan the chamber and I immediately know he came to the same assessment I did. We're trapped here. There's no place for us to run. We're his to play with and all of us have our cards open-faced on the table.

Smoke blew from his fleshy snout and he laughs. "Little pig, little pig, let me come in," he says.

"Ummm… Not by the hair of my chinny chin chin," I mumble under my breath.

Balzuzu takes a giant step forward, his hoof purposely cracking the marble floor. "Miguel… I was wondering where you'd run off to. How horribly are the two of you prepared to die?"

Father Miguel doesn't waiver. "We are not the one's dying here today, beast. It is you who should be prepared to perish."

I have no idea what Miguel is talking about but I fucking love the bravado. They lock eyes, a stare down of biblical proportions. A long moment passes then Balzuzu breaks first.

He laughs again, mocking our pettiness. "You think you have something. You think you have a weapon you can use against me."

"I have had years to prepare for your arrival," states Miguel, matter-of-factly.

Balzuzu's wings flap and he rises above the floor, assuming a position of superiority. He laughs again, heartily. "Did you find the Spear of Destiny? The Sword of Souls? Perhaps you are holding the mystical Eye of God? Do you truly believe any of those artifacts can hurt me?"

"God banished you in the Great Flood… with something as simple as water." says Miguel.

"Ha! Do you think holy water will work on me?" says Balzuzu. "I was born in the pits of Hell, a direct descendant of Araqiel, one of the Guardians of Heaven. I am imbued with the life and death force of six-hundred-and-sixty-six tainted souls. I am a Nephilim, a teacher of war… a ruler from the ancient days of earth. There is nothing you possess that could possible cause me harm."

"I possess a belief in a greater power," answers Miguel.

"You are an old fool, Miguel. Do you think God will answer your prayers?" Balzuzu scorns, more smoke blowing from his nostrils. "Do you think God will come down from his perch and save you? If God is your greater power then I will send you to him now."

"Not God. The power of the United States Military," says Miguel, yanking the canvas covering to the ground, revealing what's beneath it.

It's a large weapon, one I've seen before when my pa gave me a tour of a battleship. It's a RIM-116 rolling airframe missile launcher that's bolted to the floor for extra support and loaded to the teeth with 21 fire-and-forget missiles, meaning once they're launched they don't need any additional guidance instructions. Miguel uncurls his fist. In his palm is the RAM's remote controller. He already has Balzuzu locked in as the target. "Now I'm going to blow a lot more than smoke up your ass," Miguel says.

He fires and I see the momentary flicker of fear in Balzuzu's eyes before the missile strikes him square in the chest, not even giving him a chance to move. The rocket carries the devil through the roof of the church and outside into the bright daylight. Rubble and debris rain down on us. A second later, the missile explodes.

"Holy—" I mutter. Father Miguel's gaze stops me before I get to the second word. "You did it. You killed him."

Miguel shakes his head. "Balzuzu is nearly indestructible. He sustains himself off the souls of others and unfortunately he has a near infinite supply. I am most certain he isn't dead. I'm not even one hundred percent certain he can be dead. However, I believe we can injure him enough to force him from our world. Were you able to attach the transmitter to him?" he asks me.

The transmitter? It clicks… *'The higher calling'.* Cute. Now I know what the metal strip is. I nod.

"Good," says Miguel. "These missiles combine Sidewinder and Stinger technology. They are designed to automatically hone in on a target using infrared heat-seeking guidance or radio frequencies or in this case, my transmitter." He twists a knob on the remote control and the RAM launcher system tilts upwards. Then he fires off a second missile. "Let us pray," he adds.

I smirk. "You may make a good Catholic out of me yet, Father."

He takes that as his cue to fire off a third. The whoosh as the missile leaves its cylindrical housing is indeed the sound of a greater power. I exit through the rear door hoping to catch a glimpse of the lord's handiwork, though the grotesque scene that greets me has nothing to do with him. The werewolves have seized the advantage and are making mincemeat out of the zombies. They're tearing through them as savagely as a wood chipper does a tree. Dead body parts fly around like confetti at a parade. The bright side is, I'm glad to see the surviving townsfolk fighting side by side with them, guns blazing', doing their best to help out. I don't spot my pa or Silver Joe in the chaos—not good—but Rebel's out there working out his aggression, doing just fine.

Two more vibrating blasts come from inside the church as two more RIM's break through the roof. Father Miguel isn't taking any chances. I scan the skies looking for the big red bastard. I don't see him at first but the path the missiles take tell me where to look. I see Balzuzu ascending into the sky about a half mile to the west. From this distance, the way his wings are spread along with the long angular shape of his face, he resembles a dragon, one that's out for revenge and coming to burn our village to the ground.

The second missile approaches him from above. The devil dives downward then makes a ninety degree turn a few feet above ground. The missile turns with him, but can't match the abrupt change in direction and explodes against the ground. Balzuzu's coming back this way fast and hard, low and angry. Two more missiles bear down on him from up high. Balzuzu zig-zags, but he's still heading right for us. If these missiles don't hit him, if he somehow avoids them, then every one of us is dead. I head out into the street, ready my gun, just in case. Not that it's going to stop him, but I'd rather go out shooting a gun than standing around waiting to be slaughtered.

Balzuzu avoids the next missile by darting quickly to his left. It too explodes upon impact with the earth, throwing balls of flame into the background. Balzuzu veers back on course, narrowly avoiding the last missile as well. The plume of fire that shoots up feels symbolic, a final candle burning before our lives get snuffed out.

I kneel and ready my weapon, hoping that somehow I manage a lucky shot. I try to get one of his eyes lined up in my scope. I figure I have about ten seconds to lock in on it and take the shot. I catch his face in the scope. A portion of his long mouth is missing. Black blood drips from his chest. At least there's comfort in knowing we put a dent in him before we died. I put an ounce of pressure on the trigger, trying to lineup his eye in the crosshairs.

Then the church explodes from the inside out.

Three missiles burst forth, shot at ground level, all in a straight line on a direct collision course with our devil. Balzuzu sees me. He sees them. His eyes narrow. He wants me more than he wants to dodge them, so he doesn't change course until it's too late. He darts upward but there's no way in hell he can avoid the missiles. They arc up with him, matching and surpassing his speed. The first one blasts into his midsection, exploding into an all-consuming ball of flame. A micro second later, the next two hit him just as hard. The explosion blows me back off my feet. The weapon I was holding slides down the street. My ears ring. Still, I get a good glimpse and the results are epic.

Balzuzu took the full brunt of the triple blast and got thrown a good distance before plunging to the ground like a flaming meteor. When he hit, he created a smoldering impact crater ten yards wide. If he were truly born in the pits of hell, I'm guessing right about now he feels at home. With a little luck we sent him out the same way he came in.

A hand clasps my shoulder before I'm on my feet. It's Miguel.

"I'm okay." I nod.

"Let us pray the devil is not," he responds.

Miguel helps me to my feet. I pick up my fully automatic; make sure the locking mechanism is in place. "Let's go over there and find out."

We walk toward the crater, cautious but with a deliberate pace. We reach the edge. Flames are still burning in the middle of it like an Olympic torch. A broken wing breaches the flame. We collectively hold our breath. A thick, dark red colored hand reaches out of the fire. Then, slowly, Balzuzu stumbles forward.

He's a shell of himself, the left side of his body fully exposed, a collection of thick, fleshy muscle tissue hanging from charcoal bones. He's hemorrhaging fluid everywhere, as if he was drowning in a sea of his own black blood. His right arm is hanging useless, broken like a toy doll whose arm's twisted backwards from the elbow down. His once terrifying goat face no longer has a bottom jaw. His remaining horn is a jagged stump. Syrupy ooze drips from his eye sockets. But still he sees us. He makes it two steps forward before dropping to one knee.

"I will kill you both. Slowly. Painfully. I will imprison your souls for eternity. I will fill your infinite death with a thousand forms of torture. I will—"

I reload a brand new clip and hold down the trigger until every bullet lodges into whatever's left of his face. The barrage of incendiary lead chips away his teeth. His agonizing shrill scream becomes a choking gurgle as spongy pieces of his foul tongue dislodge and slip down his throat.

"Now that's what I call opening up a can of shut the fuck up," I say proudly.

Still, the fucker lives. I discharge the empty magazine and start searching for another.

He glares at us with what little he's got left. His words come out weak, slurred. "I will be back… for you, for everyone. Evil never dies." Then he pushes off the ground, flying weakly off into the distance.

By the time I lock the magazine in, he's out of range. Miguel grabs my wrist. "He's going back home, back through the portal. He will heal himself with new souls. We must go back to the graveyard now. Close the portal. Lock him on the other side. I can do it."

I stare at Miguel then look up once more as Balzuzu fades in the distance. That fucker killed my brother, destroyed my town, and threatened to wipe mankind from existence. *'I will be back,'* he said. Those words mull around in my noggin. Fuck that! We hurt him good, but not good enough. I have to make sure he *never* comes back, that he never *can* come back. I have to put him down for good. For my brother, for Los Agros, and for the world.

"Fine," I say to Miguel. "We'll go back to the portal. We'll close it. But first I have some things to get and some things to do."

Miguel looks at me with a worried expression, as if he can read my mind. "What are you thinking, Silas? Where are you going?"

I look at him with pure determination in my eye. Then I answer. "I'm thinking this isn't over. I'm going to Hell to kill him once and for all."

19

Miguel and I are in the basement of the house I grew up in, or as Pa calls it 'the Hill family arsenal'. Over the years we've compiled enough weapons to fully stock a small army. Easily more than enough firepower to overthrow a third world country. We obtained much of it through less than legal means, but Sheriff Martaan never cared because on days like this, when the world we lived in went to shit, Martaan knew he was going to need all the help he could get. I can tell by the empty spaces on the racks that my pa and Martaan came here first and took as much as they could carry to properly arm the townsfolk. They took a lot of stuff, but not all. There are still plenty of goodies left to choose from.

Before we came here, Martaan assured us he could handle things until the military arrived. Pa was unconscious but alive. A medical technician checking his vitals told us he'd live. My pa's as tough a man as you'll find. Even the beating he took from Balzuzu wasn't enough to make this a good day for him to die. I caught a glimpse of Silver Joe and Rebel too. Joe wasn't moving too well. The ass kicking Balzuzu gave was one he'd remember. Rebel, meanwhile, was coordinating and commanding others in his pack and making shredded wheat out of the zombies. They didn't need my help. The best thing I could do for any of them was to finish the job we started. Balzuzu needed to die. I need to choose the best weapons from my arsenal to make that a reality.

I haven't been down here in a while. It takes me a few minutes to re-familiarize myself with the layout. I scan the room; handheld pistols, machine guns, flamethrowers—Martaan should have grabbed those—, knives… finally I spot the truly explosive stuff. It took four missiles just to knock the wind out of Balzuzu's sails. But since I can't carry a RIM-116 rolling airframe missile launcher on my back, I need something portable, yet even more effective.

I turn to Father Miguel, "Talk to me. Tell me everything you know."

"That would take years. I've spent a lifetime studying them," Miguel says sardonically.

"Cliff notes. Start with fuckface. What's a Nephilim?"

Miguel paces a moment. I could tell it was a big story and he was figuring out how to condense it down to size. He gets there and begins. "Many millennia ago a group of watcher angels were dispatched to Earth to watch over humanity."

Normally I tune out at hearing religious stuff like this, but I've seen enough in the last few hours to keep my trap shut.

Miguel continues. "However, instead of simply watching us, they decided to do *more*. They chose to guide us in their ways, teaching us things we would have been better off not knowing. They taught us the art of war, the use of weaponry and sorcery for untoward purposes. They also desired us, procreating among us. They bore children. Their offspring, the end result of this unholy union between god-like beings and women, were the Nephilim, a race of giants brimming with savagery and power who followed no laws but their own. The children of the watchers became our conquerors. Araqiel was one of the first Nephilim. Balzuzu is one of his sons."

"Still alive after all this time?" I ask.

"They are not like us. They do not abide by the laws of God. They are immortal. Eventually, God had enough of their destructive ways so he directly intervened on behalf of mankind, something he rarely does. He banished the Nephilim from Earth with a great flood. Sent them to another realm."

"God banished them to Hell?"

"Not exactly," answers Miguel. "Hell is merely the space between. Do you believe in souls, Silas?"

"I don't think too much about it," I say.

"And yet you are one of the purest souls I have ever encountered. I have known that since I baptized you. Balzuzu noticed it the moment he lifted you off the ground in the graveyard. I could see it in his eyes. He let you live so he could taint you."

A wry grin crossed my lips. "Forgive me, Father, but I'm pretty fucking far from being a saint."

"Yet you confront evil every time you encounter it with a bravery few men have ever shown."

"Well someone needs to kick them in the balls." I shrug.

"That's an accurate, but most ineloquent way to put it," he says. "All living things have a soul, Silas. It's what defines us… what makes us who we are."

"Even werewolves? Even zombies?"

"Even Balzuzu," he responds. "But theirs are *captured* souls. When a human is born he or she is gifted from God a perfectly pure soul. It is a thing of utter beauty, utter perfection. As that person grows, their actions color that soul. When they sin—and I'm talking about true sins that come from bad intentions;

deceiving, stealing, murdering—their souls become tainted. When that person dies, their soul leaves this realm and travels to God's kingdom. And I mean truly travels from our plane of existence into the next. If that soul is still pure enough, it will return to God an untouchable invisible light along a dark path. If that soul is tainted, it becomes vulnerable to those who inhabit the space along the path… the space *between*."

"You mean between Heaven and Earth. So Hell is whatever lies along that path and that's where God banished the Nephilim to," I say just to clarify.

"Yes. The more tainted the soul, the easier it is for the Nephilim to capture it. Only God has power over a pure soul. Only God can contain that power. But once a soul is tainted its power is reduced and then any devil living along the path can claim it, hijack it if you will, and twist it for their own sinister purposes."

"I'm not sure I'm following that part," I say, trying to get a better understanding.

"Think of a pure soul as a burning sphere. Only God's hands are powerful enough to hold it. Think of tainted souls as spheres that have cooled off. Now less powerful hands can grab onto them. As there are many sins, souls are cooled off in many different ways. There are a diversity of devils inhabiting the paths between here and God's Kingdom. Each one has a different specialty. They look for souls with certain temperatures. Balzuzu goes for the coldest. His lust for the worst of the worst among us knows no bounds."

"So if your soul is pure you go to Heaven. If you have committed sins, depending on the level of those sins, your soul may be claimed by a devil, essentially sentencing that soul to their own personal hell."

"We try our best to keep people on the right path. This is why," replies Miguel.

"What do they do with the souls they capture?"

"Anything they want," he answers. "It depends on the devil that has it. Some are tortured, others are studied and used for trade. The fortunate few are given a chance at redemption."

"And in Balzuzu's case?" I ask, getting straight to the point.

"Balzuzu has the ability to reshape those souls and move them across vast distances, across realms. He has the ability to send those souls back into our world in various forms. He is incredibly powerful and he has collected a great many souls. He has been using them to build monster armies that have not only helped him escape from the underworld but also to be used to rule once he got here. Balzuzu himself created the werewolf species by placing tainted human souls inside of the bodies of real wolves and reshaping their DNA with a touch of sorcery. That's why some of these wolves remember who they were when they were human. That's also how he was able to animate an army of the dead. He simply shifted hundreds of the souls under his control into the corpses in the graveyard."

"And voila… instant zombie army. Nice!"

"The Book of Jude states that the watchers themselves are bound in the valleys of the earth until Judgment Day. I believe Balzuzu is trying to bring that about."

"Fuckin A. All the more reason to stop him forever." I tilt my head to the multitude of weapons, realizing that even with everything Miguel just told me, none of it helps me put Balzuzu down for good. "So what do you suggest I bring?"

"Whatever you can carry," replies Miguel.

20

I dress myself in the fireproof thermal suit my pa had specially made for me years ago when he met me in Romania to hunt dragons. It's made of lightweight vermiculite to withstand temperatures of up to 2000 degrees and comes with its own closed circuit self-contained breathing apparatus to let me rebreathe my own air. I have a duffel made of the same material which should be enough to get me, and whatever I can fit in there, through the portal without bursting into flames.

I start packing. I've learned firsthand that a direct confrontation with Balzuzu is a losing proposition. Still, I grab some night-time hunting supplies, a couple of long daggers, and my Lupara, simply because I feel naked without them. I know this job requires destructive efficiency, something that gives me a huge bang for the buck and won't take up a lot of space, weapons that are portable, easy to carry. That simplifies my choices.

I grab close to a dozen grenades then load up the rest of the duffel with all the Composition C-4 it can hold. Both have minimal risk of being accidentally set off, and most importantly, they both blow shit up. Hopefully the opportunity will arise to shove one right up Balzuzu's asshole. I grab some customized blasting caps, code them into the remote detonator, and place the entire triggering package in insulated pockets.

I look around to see if there's anything else I can use. I see Miguel holding the Super Bazooka. It's an M20. It weighs twelve pounds and breaks into two parts. The High Explosive Anti-Tank rockets weigh about eight pounds each. Unfortunately, I can't take that with me as well.

"You should throw that in the truck, just in case he comes back through," I say.

Miguel nods. "I will. Hopefully, it won't be necessary."

A few moments later, we're in the front seat of Miguel's pickup truck. The Harley's in the back along with everything I plan to bring with me. We're fully loaded, heading back to the graveyard… literally on a road to Hell.

"So, what do you think it's like down there?" I ask.

"Can't say," says Miguel. "Never been. Never met someone who has."

His response triggered something I hadn't really thought about before. Balzuzu, Miguel, and my father all had a past. A past that involved Balzuzu killing my brother. If he did come through the portal six years ago, he didn't seem like the type to just kill and go back. I'm fairly certain he would have stayed. Miguel veers off the road and the car bounces onto a path that skirts the woods.

"How exactly did Balzuzu kill my brother?" I ask.

"That's a discussion you need to have with your father. He would want it that way."

"It's been years. If he wanted it that way, I would know by now."

He stares at me for a beat, deciding if he should reveal what happened. Then he says, "Today was the first time in millennia Balzuzu's physical body was able to break into our plane of existence. But he doesn't need to be here physically to wreak havoc. Aside from shifting the souls of others into new bodies, occasionally he shifts his own."

"Demonic possession," I mutter.

"Yes," responds Miguel. "It is not something he would do lightly as it renders his real body vulnerable. It is only something he would do with great purpose. Your father hunted evil, too. Not exactly the same kind you do. Humans, but no less monstrous. There was an African warlord that went by the name

Kubla Kotise, a savage man responsible for unthinkable acts, many of which were against women and children. He prevailed against every attempt to stop him. He claimed to work specifically for the devil. Your father went off grid one night with a small band of Marines and ended his reign of terror once and for all. But something that happened on that mission spooked him. After encountering Kubla, he believed he spoke the truth. Your father brought back with him religious artifacts that he found on Kubla's person and showed them to me. They were dark, mystical objects that no man should be in contact with. One was a ruby with 'The eye of the devil' inscribed on it in Latin. I recognized it immediately as a summoning device. Kubla wasn't lying when he said he worked for the devil."

"Balzuzu," I say, knowing it's not much of a leap.

Father Miguel nodded. "The mystical ruby allowed them to communicate with each other. What I didn't realize at the time was that there were two rubies. You're father only gave me one. The other he kept… I think as a reminder to himself that there was true evil in the world. A few months later your mother and father were hiking in the woods. Out of nowhere they were attacked by a bear. Your mother was mauled, near death. There wasn't anyone around for miles. There was no way humanly possible for your father to save her. So, in desperation, he used the ruby he kept to contact the devil. The devil offered him a deal. He would save your mother if your father gave up a piece of his soul.

"Of course your father thought he was talking about his own soul. So he eagerly accepted the deal. He loved your mother very deeply, still does. The thought of sacrificing himself to save her wasn't even a thought at all. However, what he didn't know was that when two people who love each other make a child, as well as the physical, a piece of each of their souls is passed along. Your father unknowingly sold your brother's soul to the devil instead of his. Another day, when your father and brother were hunting in the woods, Balzuzu possessed the demon bear again and claimed your brother.

"In the church that day, I immediately realized what happened. Both bear attacks were no mere coincidences. It was Balzuzu's revenge. Kubla Kotise was one of Balzuzu's human assets. Your father took him from Balzuzu. Balzuzu then plotted to take something from your father in return. He personally transferred his own soul into the bear, possessed the creature, committed the attack, and quickly returned back to his realm. When your father confessed what he had done to your mother, how he saved her, she never forgave him for it. That is why she left. That is why your father became an alcoholic. Balzuzu broke him that day. He has never recovered. I used the ruby I had. I contacted the devil, looked into his eyes, and told him I would make him pay for what he had done. He told me he was coming. I have been preparing for him ever since."

21

We take the truck as far as we can then park it and ride through the woods on the motorcycle. It doesn't take us long to reach the gate and we dismount right beside the otherworldly portal. A loud cacophony of odd pops and whooshing noises emanate from it like a ghostly warning. Flames erupt off its dark surface like solar flares off the sun, the air above it bubbles like boiling water.

As we stare into the reality of what I'm about to do, Father Miguel says, "Perhaps now might be a good time to change your mind."

I pick up a rock and toss it into the abyss. It drops about fifteen feet then makes a small popping sound as it disappears beneath an upcoming jet of flame. I'm not sure if the rock simply disintegrated or exploded into nothingness. "Fuck it," I say.

"*It* seems to be a particularly pointless and painful way to die," says Miguel.

"You said God banished them to the other side with a flood. That means they lived when they were washed through. If they can make it, so can I."

"Do I need to explain to you how completely illogical that is?" asks Miguel. It's a rhetorical question that doesn't need an answer. "They are far more resilient creatures."

I ignore the logic. "Pass me the rope." I put the protective helmet with the clear facemask on, making myself look like a spaceman. Miguel grabs the rope off the back of the bike and tosses it to me. I unravel it, get right to the edge, and slowly lower it into the hellhole. Flames reach out for it like slicing knives but it's too heavily coated to burn. I give it more slack and the abyss crackles in response. A firestorm whips around it, ascending the twine with a flare that shoots upward at lightning speed. The hellfire coils around me before I fall back out of its grasp then the flame dissipates into nothingness. To my credit, I still have a death grip on the rope which suddenly goes taut in my hands. For a second it's like the pull of a fishing rod with a great white shark on the other end but then it immediately relaxes and the eruptions below die down. I get to my feet, untoasted, my end of the rope still in hand.

"It appears your way down just got cut off," says Miguel, slightly pleased.

He thinks the lower part of the rope is gone, either severed in half or in cinders. It certainly must have appeared that way. But he's wrong. "Sorry, father. Check this out." I pull the rope up. At first there's some tension that requires a modicum of effort then it's practically weightless and I easily gather it up like a fishing line dipped in a pond. I show Miguel the far end, the one that slipped through to the other side. It's slightly charred but otherwise right as rain. "What enters the abyss only appears to go poof." I blow my hands up in some grand gesture. "In actuality, I believe the flames represent the chemical and physical reactions that result when something crosses the threshold between our world and theirs."

Miguel grabs the rope, examines it closely. He looks perplexed but I can tell he understands. He releases the lower half of the rope back into the fiery darkness. Another predictable burst of flame spits out, twirls around the rope, and subsides. "May God guide your way," he concedes.

"If I'm not back in a few hours, seal this gate tighter than Virgin Mary's—" Miguel's glance cuts me off. "Sorry, my brain goes to strange places sometimes. Do what you have to. And don't worry about me. If I get stuck down there, I'll just take over the whole damn place."

Miguel drives a few spikes in the ground and we make double shit sure the rope knot holds tight. I wrap the slack around my right sleeve, stand with my back to the edge, and in one giant leap for mankind, I repel down the side. A fireball erupts to my right but the suit protects me. I kick off the wall, drop a few feet, repeat the pattern until at about twenty feet deep I pass through something that feels like a bubble of jelly.

Hellfire engulfs me.

I plunge.

Then my world literally turns upside down.

22

I lie there, flat on the hard surface, totally disoriented, nauseous to the point where I have the uncontrollable urge to hurl. I try to keep what little food I've eaten down where it belongs, but soon I'm spraying the inside of my clear facemask with chunks of last night's beef stew. The contained smell is so vile I hurl again and again, until there's nothing left but dry heaves.

I immediately lose the helmet, not even allowing my brain to process all the things that could go bad when I do. Extreme temperature, no oxygen, poison air… all pale in comparison to death by being locked in an airtight suit asphyxiated by my own vomit. I breathe in. Deep. Amazed at the fact that's there's something to breathe in at all. Somehow, I'm inhaling oxygen. There is air here. It comes with a slight charcoal aftertaste but it's air just the same.

I look around and realize my arrival point is just the tip of a hell-fucked iceberg. The landscape is so alien I might as well be on another planet. For all I know, maybe I am. Glowing blood-colored stone make up the surface for as far as I can see, which isn't all that far. Canyon-like walls made of the same stone climb into pure darkness. Yet, I can tell I'm not in a large cavern. The utter blackness is Hell's version of a sky, a void so devoid of color its presence presses down on this place like a blanket of despair.

Mossy, crystalized stalagmites of varying heights rise up from the ground, cracking upward from the stony surface like hundreds of craggily old fingers pointing to the hollow blackness above. A few of them are so tall and sharp they remind me of giant fangs. The slimy vegetation that coats them reflects the crimson-hued luminescence of the rocky ground beneath me, giving off an eerie, puke green light that bathes the entire place in misery.

The gateway to Hell is on the ground a few feet to my left. Flames swirl around it in a whirlpool pattern carried by a circular wind that brings in debris from our side, while sending the brimstone smell of this place out. That must be why there's a breathable atmosphere in a place where no one needs to breathe. A twig shoots through, rising upward like a thrown spear before getting swept aside. As it drops down next to me I get it.

Whatever comes through the portal is subject to an immediate gravity reversal. I fell through a hole, only once I was on the other side I was falling up. The whipping wind and the laws of physics, which at least somewhat mimic our own, did the rest, depositing me where I fell, like I just got off the roughest rollercoaster ride in existence. Like a sock in the dryer, I was literally flipped, tossed, spin dried, and lost.

I slap on my generation 3 autogated night vision goggles and get a slightly better view. I'm immediately greeted by my first pleasant surprise. My pa's motorcycle is lying sideways about twenty yards away. I thought for sure it exploded. That's what usually happens when fire meets a gas tank. Yet here it was, still in one piece, which is more than I can say about the half zombie underneath it. I lose the fireproof suit, arm up, and approach it. Even though it's just an upper torso, I see it's still moving so I spend a bullet putting it down for good. I lift the bike upright and race the throttle. The growl of the engine followed by the steady hum is music to my ears.

Then something louder growls behind me, a throaty bark that echoes throughout the canyon-like terrain. I turn and see a massive beast the size of a mammoth charging my way. It's wooly like one, but it has three head's; each of a wild wolfhound.

Hell's idea of a threesome seriously differs from mine.

Six vicious eyes bear down on me. Thick sharp teeth glimmer green, eager to rip me apart. I've heard stories about this beast before. Apparently, the myths are true. In order for a living being to enter Hell he must get past the Devil's guard dog; a three-headed hellhound named Cerberus who has an insatiable appetite for live meat. I can tell he's hungry. I see it in his piercing animal eyes. It's probably been a really long time since he's feasted.

And here I am, merely a bone.

23

I'm on the bike, tearing ass, zig-zagging erratically around the stalagmites like a bat in a belfry. Cerberus is right on my tail, crashing through the stalagmites between us, shattering the stony protrusions as if they were made of Legos. I feel his doggie breath on the hackles of my neck and cut a hard right around a large boulder, narrowly avoiding death as a chew toy. The big mutt skids into a wall trying to stop, colliding with it so hard pieces of the blood stone chip off. Then he twists back around and continues the chase.

My wheels have a good grip on the rock-like surface. I twist the bars hard right again, plant my foot on the ground as the bike banks, spin around, and dart back toward the gate. I think about luring him through the portal, but I'm not keen on dropping another big problem on Earth's lap, let alone Miguel who's standing right there. So I scout the terrain, look for a spot where at least I'll have a fighting chance. A row of tall, thick stalagmites that look like a bottom row of teeth are about a half click to my left. I go full throttle, accelerating so quickly the cycle jumps into a wheelie. When the front tire lands, rubber burns and I glance behind me. Fido's coming full blast, smashing through the smaller stalagmites, turning pillars of stone into piles of dust. I hope the ones I'm heading for are made of sturdier stuff. They're going to have to be.

Fido's running faster than my cycle, his giant strides covering a lot of ground with each step. He's gaining on me. But I see my first piece of good news. The stalags are staggered like stone trees in a forest with narrow spaces between them. I can hide in there, making his rather large size a disadvantage. I lean forward, hoping for that little bit of extra speed. Fido's behind me coming fast and hard. Neither of us plans on stopping.

I zip between two towering columns of rock. A second later, the underworld quakes as Cerebus collides hard with the thick mossy stone stalagmites. A micro-second after that, I have a more immediate problem. There's a king-size boulder right in front of me and I don't think I can stop in time… and I'm nowhere near as durable as three-face. I wildly burn a sharp left. Another 'stone tree' is right there. I cut a quick right, but the space is too tight and the bike can't compensate for my sudden change in direction. The motorcycle skids, balance is lost, and I'm thrown sideways, both the bike and I sliding to a hard, nasty stop. I should be broken and bleeding. Instead, I'm lying in a patch of vegetation that feels soft, sticky, and wet, like a used kitchen sponge. Whatever the shit is, I'm grateful for it. I'm alive, the Harley's still in one piece, and I've got a monster that needs killing so I can go kill the devil.

Cerberus is having a temper tantrum loud enough to wake the dead, which down here isn't a joke. He's growling up a terrifying storm and throwing his massive weight against the stalagmites between us. So far they're holding, the pillars of God if you ask me, but they won't for long. I reach into my pouch of weapons, deciding to save the heavy artillery for Balzuzu and reach for the Lupara. I race toward the rocks he's pounding on. There's a loud crash. It rains pebbles then one of his heads is through. A mouth darts at me, its jaws snapping shut an inch before my face. I pull back from the nice shiny teeth and fire into his maw. Fangs shatter. I fire again. This head retreats, but another crashes through the bloodstone and attacks me from the side.

Its snout knocks me down. A giant paw smashes through another stalagmite, tries to squash me flat. I roll, turn, and fire another blast into a face that comes far too close for comfort.

The third head appears out of nowhere. I run then hide between three colossal stalagmites set in a triangular pattern. Cerberus reaches my makeshift fortress in one stride and with a sharp movement knocks the top half off two of the three stalagmites, showing me just how futile my efforts to hide truly are. I reload and fire, hitting him multiple times in his front right leg, hoping to hobble him. It doesn't.

Another head comes from the side taking out the top half of the last stalagmite. The big dog has me pinned, the massive beast hovering above me. I'm a sitting duck trapped like dog food in a bowl made of three stony stumps. All that's left is for him to decide which mouth feeds on me first. Fuck waiting for Balzuzu. Cerberus takes two seconds to decide it'll be the middle head that eats me. In that first second, I grab a grenade and pull the pin. The following second the grenade is heading for the open mouth before it heads towards me.

The grenade skips off his slick tongue, bounces to the roof of his mouth, and detonates. The result is awe inspiring. The middle head bursts like a water balloon. Gooey inside-the-skull stuff spatters the surrounding stalagmites, me, and his other two heads. The only thing left in the middle is a fleshy stump that looks like it was pelted with tomatoes.

But I've been in the game long enough to know this is only a good beginning. Monsters, especially giant ones, never go down easy. Not for one second do I think this devil dog is going to be any different. It kicks up on its rear legs in pain, shock, and anger. I pull the pin from another grenade. One in the mouth was lucky. This one I roll underneath him towards his rear legs. The left head lurches towards me, snarling, coming fast. My grenade explodes before it gets the chance to snap down. Its right rear leg is blown clean off and the massive mutt hound stumbles sideways.

I don't stop. I lob two more at its exposed underbelly. In return, I get a gut bath that's equal in nastiness as to when I upchucked in my space suit. The smell is revolting, abhorrent. Ten times worse than all the other rotten odors I've been saddled with today, a hundred times worse than the shit pile I hid in last night. A piece of his large intestine drapes over my shoulder. Or maybe it's his small intestine because he's such a large dog. I gag then realize something soft and spongy is in my mouth. I dry heave again. Twice. The price of victory.

I wipe my eyes with my sleeve and see the big beast. It's writhing. Both of its heads are still moving. Then one of the heads howls, a roar so powerful it shakes the foundations of Hell.

When it stops, its four remaining eyes lock onto me with a gaze so intense I know I'll be paying for this for an eternity. Not even my death will satisfy this creature's bloodlust for revenge. So, fuck it. I figure I'll get my money's worth. I grab another grenade, pull the pin, and toss it in the quiet head's mouth. Then I race by the noisy head, and as he weakly snaps his jaw at me, I shove another live grenade in its wet nostril.

I race as fast as I can and take cover behind a stalag stump. I hear two consecutive booms then patiently wait a few seconds to avoid being hit with any more of his brain matter. I listen to the sucking sound as his doggie parts go splat on Hell's floor, finding it as soothing to my ears as Mozart. When the symphony ends, I peek out, see the mess I made, and all I can think of is it's a shame I wasn't able to watch.

Hell's a horrifying, fucked up place. I'm beginning to like it down here. Now all I gotta do is find Balzuzu and figure out how to kill him now that I'm out of grenades.

24

I gather up the bike and walk it out of the stalagmite forest. The terrain is starting to feel familiar. I just need to figure out which way to go to find Balzuzu. I hop on and gun the cycle in the direction Cerberus came from, figuring if he's the guard dog there must be something in that direction worth guarding. After a mile it feels like I'm on a trail to nowhere. The entire place looks the same, a boring kaleidoscope of nauseating deep hues reflecting over a canyon of emptiness under the weight of an unforgiving black sky. Maybe that's what Hell is supposed to be, a void filled with nothing, a desolate chasm of hopelessness.

I take it slow, look around, and continually check my six for any nasty surprises. You never know what else inhabits a place like this. Then something taps my noggin like a bug on a windshield… *only this bug slips inside.* It's almost imperceptibly light, but I feel it mingling with my mind. My brain tingles. An image flashes. The body of a man hacked to pieces. A face of a husky man with a beard reflects in the pool of blood. Two more invisible 'bugs' zap my forehead and make themselves at home inside my head. More images, more memories that aren't mine. A machine gun fires and multiple bodies fall lifeless into an open pit. Dark skinned hands lower the gun then a faceless man spits into a mass grave. A flash of red and I'm elsewhere. A seedy motel. A degenerate blond, young but aged well past her years, stares at her hollow face in the mirror. Behind her is the man she purposely overdosed so she could steal his share of crystal meth.

I hit the brakes so I don't crash as the horrible images overwhelm me. More zaps. It's like I got too close to a beehive and the stings won't stop, each one bringing with it memories of a life filled with evil deeds. Sex slaves being drugged, used, and locked up. A tattooed Asian man being gutted with a sword. A middle-eastern man ordering death. A bank robber shooting a hostage. A drug deal that goes violently wrong. It continues… a montage of wicked acts, including the sounds, smells, and tastes of the worst things that men and women could do to each other and I can't turn it off.

"Just focus on my thoughts," a voice calls out from within me.

I do. I see a slim piece of metal slip between the driver's side window and the door panel of a soon to be stolen car. A fist fight with a drunk in a bar. There someone else's bad memories, but they don't nearly rise to the level of evil as the crimes committed by the others. Not even close. I concentrate, forcing myself to stay with them. I see me as a boy, but through someone else's eyes. Positive emotions flood forward, the horrible imagery fading away.

"They're gone. Your soul burns too bright. They can't stay for long." I recognize the voice immediately.

"Christian?" I ask, just to make sure.

"Yeah, dipshit, it's me… your brother. Miss me?"

25

I don't answer. I don't know what to say.

"My, my… look how much you've grown," he says. "Okay, not much. So tell me… what the fuck are you doing here?"

"Wow… if you weren't dead and already in Hell, I'd tell you you're still an asshole," I reply. Then I answer his question. "Balzuzu's pissed me off. I'm here to kick his teeth in."

He chuckles. I remember that laugh. I miss it. "Man…" he starts, "So… you didn't come all this way to see me."

"Sorry, bro. I never imagined."

He laughs again. "You don't ever quit, do you? Damn… reminds me of the time I put a laxative in your chocolate milk then followed it up by lacing the toilet paper with itching powder. You hunted me down for three straight days, never quit looking for revenge until you finally got it by replacing the toothpaste in my tube with bird shit."

"Took you a week to realize it too," I proudly add.

"You gave as good as you got," he says.

"Whatever happened when I put mayonnaise in your jock strap at school?"

"Fuck… that was you? I thought that was Bobby Larkowski after I got a blowjob from his sister."

"Really… Tammy? She didn't seem like the type."

"No, not her. His older sister, Jamie Lynn," he says.

I laugh hard. "Bobby didn't have an older sister. Jamie's his ma."

"No way. Damn, she was smokin' hot… and very talented. I bragged about that score for weeks."

"Do tell. No wonder he hated your guts," I chuckle.

"Man… shits and giggles. Those were good times." He pauses a moment. His tone becomes more somber. "I saw how badly you messed up Balzuzu. Nice work."

"Nobody fucks with the Hill brothers," I say.

"Amen to that, brother."

"But I've got to be honest. It was mostly Father Miguel that kicked his ass. I'm just here to finish the job."

"Then I've got bad news for you. You're running a fool's errand. Balzuzu's not like us, he's not like ordinary monsters. The devil can't be killed."

"He's not *the* devil. And bullshit," I protest. "Everything dies."

"He doesn't. That's why I tried to stop him before he broke through.

"Yeah… and how does a disembodied soul do that?"

My brother goes silent again, a pause that lingers long enough to where I wonder if he'll ever be coming back. Then his voice returns. "Fine, I'll tell you. But promise me you won't take it to heart."

"Take what to heart?" I question.

"Dad pissed off Balzuzu something good. Out of revenge, Balzuzu took me. Heck… I figure I was headed here anyway, just not so soon… you know."

"You weren't. Father Miguel says only the worst of the worst end up here."

"Either way, I was on the path," Christian says. "Father Miguel did his best to right me, but I let him down each and every time. Anyhow, Balzuzu had fun with me for a long while. He played with me the way a cat does a mouse. He tortured me until I couldn't feel anything anymore, ripped my soul to pieces. Then he'd put me back together just so he could do it all over again. Can't even remember anymore how many times.

"The final time, though, was different. He was molding me, changing me, trying to forge me into something different… something more in his image. He spent a long time breaking me. Suddenly, he started rebuilding me. When he was done, he shifted my soul top side into the body of a werewolf, made me a card-carrying member of his evil army. He thought it would be the ultimate irony, me racing into town with the pack to kill my father. He just didn't realize I'm more stubborn than a billy goat after lunch. All he did was make me mad."

My eyes widen. I see where this is going and I'm not sure whether to kick myself into next week or drown my sorrow in a bottomless bottle of Jack.

Christian continues. "We all knew his plan. We were all part of it. Balzuzu was going topside, this time personally, to take humanity to task for every fucked up thing it ever did. He promised that fuckwad Frank Jones immortality for his family if he willingly sacrificed himself to open the gate. That stupid fuck was going along with it, knowing full well what Balzuzu planned to do, how many millions he planned to kill. I had a counter plan. I went into town, gutted the old prick—heck, that fuck deserved to die—then I left him like that as a warning to dad as to who and what was behind it all. Apparently, you got there first."

"Oh my god… I killed you," I mutter. "I sent you back here to this godforsaken place. Why didn't you tell me?"

"Cause then you never would have killed me. I wasn't living as no werewolf. No way I was going to play any part in what he had planned. I wanted to come back here. I wanted Balzuzu to know that no matter what he did to me, I would never belong to him. I didn't care if he tortured me for all eternity. It would have all been worth it for that one moment I saw he knew what I did and I got to spit in his face. And then, every time he'd come to torture me, I could laugh at his ugly mug knowing that no matter what he did to me, ultimately I got the better of him. Every time he looked at me, he would stare into the face of his own failure."

"You're as vengeful a prick as I am," I say.

"You betcha," he replies.

"Then I stumbled into the graveyard like a fool and fucked everything up."

"Yeah, but seeing what you did to him, I'd call it even."

"Not yet, it's not," I add.

"You know… I was gonna lead you back to the gateway, get you the fuck outta dodge."

"Fuck that." I say defiantly.

"Fucking right, fuck that. I'll take you to his home. I still don't think we can kill that asshole, but maybe we could find a way to put mayonnaise in his jock strap."

26

I'm riding the bike. My brother's riding shotgun in my head. My load's a lot lighter now that we've strategically placed half the C-4.

"I have no idea if any of this is going to work. If it doesn't, take the bike and get the fuck out of here," says Christian.

"And what about you?"

"I'm stuck here no matter how this thing plays out. By the way, how did you get by Cerberus? That dog takes shits bigger than you."

"Let's just say Balzuzu's going to need more than a pooper scooper to clean up that mess," I tell him.

"You are amazing, little bro. Larger than life. Don't ever forget that. How's Dad?"

"Not to stay on the subject but shitty… and that's when he has his head out of the bottle. He never got over what happened. Now I see why."

"Tell him it's okay. I understand. I know he didn't know. I never blamed him. Tell him I love him and I forgive him."

I nod.

"How's Mom?" he asks.

"Mom left. Took off shortly after what happened."

"She must blame him too. Tell her not too. Balzuzu has ways about him. I've seen that fuck twist lifelong saints into sinners in under an hour and those were on days he was bored. He took his time plotting how to hurt us the most. No one could have spotted his deceptions. It's not Dad's fault. Make sure she knows that."

"I will."

The canyon-like walls narrow and the stones blacken. The rock valley reeks of death. At the end is an immense cocoon, almost hive-like but with a shell of solid granite, pock marked at varying heights with multiple tunnels that presumably lead inside. A few of the entrances are accessible at ground level.

"This is his house, if you can call it that," Christian says.

"Lovely. The place could really use a woman's touch. A little Arm & Hammer wouldn't hurt either," I say, repulsed by the pungent scent.

"I couldn't tell ya," my brother replies. "Us disembodied souls don't have noses."

"Well, trust me. A dragon fart would improve the smell of this place."

"It is Hell."

"Which entrance should I take?"

"All roads lead to Balzuzu. But the one in the middle is the most direct. Set more C-4 charges here and here," he says.

He can't point, but in my mind I see exactly where he wants me to place them. I follow his instructions to the letter, insert the blasting caps, and double check the coded triggering mechanism so they won't explode until they receive the correct signal from the remote detonator I'm holding. I just need to be within twenty yards to be good to blow.

"Leave the bike here. The terrain in there gets a little rough.

I hop off and lean the cycle against a wall. We enter the wide tunnel. It's straight but the ground is jagged and bumpy. The further we walk the worse the smell gets. After about twenty yards, I can't even see the reflective glow of the crimson stone outside. It's pitch black. I wouldn't be able to see a thing without my night vision goggles. My brother instructs me where to stick more C-4.

"What's he doing in there?" I ask.

"He's gathering. You weakened him severely. He heals by filling himself with new souls."

"You've seen this before?" I ask, wondering how he would know that. "Have you or the other tortured souls ever fought back?"

My brother laughs. "We would need arms and legs for that… can't do more than buzz in his ear. We're at his mercy, completely helpless. But he's not the only devil down here. Occasionally, they fight."

The Nephilim. "Great! What do they fight about?"

"Souls, who can claim what, territory; they're a notoriously greedy lot, not big on sharing."

We walk a little further. I set more charges. My brother's plan is simple; we get to the lair, get his attention, lure him into the tunnel, run like the world is about to blow up, then blow up his world. With luck his entire house will collapse and bury him for a long, long time.

But it's not enough for me.

"Where do the other tunnels lead?" I ask.

"A few lead to the far side of his lair. Some lead above. Others branch off to different parts of this lovely establishment."

Above. "Show me," I say, as I reverse course and start walking back outside to where we came from.

"Whoa. What are you thinking, little bro? Whatever it is, I already don't like it."

"It ain't a fight until someone gets punched in the face. You taught me that. If anyone needs a punch in the face, it's Fuckzuzu."

"Don't get crazy. Even in his weakened state, if he gets a hand on you, he'll snap you in half."

"Well, I'm already halfway to heaven," I say.

We're back outside. I scan the multiple tunnels. "Which goes up?" My brother remains silent. "If you don't tell me, I'll just pick one."

"There," my brother responds. I can hear the reluctance in his voice as he mentally directs me.

"This is where you get off. Looking at how thick this place is, there's a chance he doesn't know I'm here. But he may sense your soul. Your presence might give me away."

Both of us realize this is goodbye. "God speed, little bro. Don't forget to tell ma and pa I love them. And I love you, too. And when you see Balzuzu, give him one from me."

I feel a light sting then my brother's gone.

"Love you too, big bro," I mutter.

I slip inside the tunnel knowing that somehow I have to kill Balzuzu. Even if Miguel can seal the portal forever and protect the Earth, the big red fuck is still going to be around to torture my brother's soul for eternity. That's something I can't allow. The path slants upward then hits a wall. I grab hold of the jutted rock, get a good grip, and start to climb. Balzuzu and I are due for another face to face.

27

I reach the top, my hand grips the ledge, and I pull myself up. There's another wide tunnel here that digs inward on a downward slope about twenty degrees. I follow it. It takes a descending spiral, bringing me to the far end of the cocoon. The stone is slicker here, coated with something dark, wet, and sticky that vaguely resembles black jelly. The air is thicker and brings with it a stronger brimstone aftertaste. The quicker I'm out of here the better.

I run multiple strategies through my head, realizing that each and every one of them is useless. All the C-4 I brought with me is carefully placed, I used all my grenades on Fido, and somewhere back in that stalagmite forest I lost my Lupara. All I have left are my two long daggers which I would like to use to cut his throat and stab his heart, except there isn't a blade sharp enough to penetrate his rhino-like hide. Add to that the problem that once I get too close to him, he'll twist my head off like a bottle cap. My brother's plan was the only one that had even a five percent chance of success. If I was less stubborn, I would climb back down and follow the original strategy, but I'll be damned to here if I'm leaving this place without sticking him with something.

There's an eerie red glow at the end of the path, an evil light at the end of a dark tunnel that leads to the gooey center of this fucked up tootsie pop. I quietly make my way to the ledge and I'm looking down into an open chamber around a quarter of the size of a football stadium where black ooze drips like moisture from hardened walls. The jelly is bubbling, pulsating, spurting out spores of black goo that looks like overheated caviar. I'm sweating, but not out of fear. The air is hot, thick, and moist like a sauna. Almost imperceptibly small lights are zipping and darting about like mosquitos. I gaze below. The floor is oval shaped, cratered in the middle, like the inside of a giant nutshell, and kneeling right in the center in a puddle of the vile black stuff is the chief nut himself, *Balzuzu*. I have to say, for a guy who is the king of his domain, he lives like shit.

His back is to me. His wings are spread and they don't look nearly as damaged as they were. A circling blue-black light makes an abrupt downward turn and races toward him. It hits his skin like a raindrop, sits there a brief moment, but instead of rolling off like a drop of water would, it absorbs into his skin like he's a sponge. Balzuzu rises, turns, a wounded hulking red beast that looks surprisingly spry for someone that could barely move just a few hours ago. His lower jaw is almost fully reformed. The scarring on his face, what's left of the bullet-holes I filled it with, makes him look even nastier then he did when he first came through the portal. I see the lateral muscle on his right side literally knitting itself together, healing rapidly right before my eyes. At this rate, he'll be back to full strength ready to terrorize us again before the day breaks.

He resumes his kneeling position in the center of the ooze. His arms spread and another light turns sharply toward him, as if he called it to him. The tiny light drop lands on his knee. He breathes deep and the light seeps inside him. He waits for a while then rises, pacing around, stretching his neck and circling his head like a boxer before a bout. When he's satisfied, he repeats the routine, kneeling once again, but this time after he absorbs a light he grabs a handful of the poisonous dark jelly and washes with it. He stops, but the black ooze keeps moving, crawling over his wounds like a thousand insects, covering his skin until it becomes part of him. I notice him grin, a look of respite. This process is soothing him, helping him heal. Every light he collects a soul that empowers him, every application of jelly a balm that repairs his powerful physical form. Every moment I watch is a moment he makes himself stronger.

So I decide to act now.

There's only one spot on his body I can think of where he might be vulnerable. I stand at the edge, my toes curling over the rim. I tighten my grip around the handles of my long daggers, holding them firmly one in each hand. My knees are bent, my legs tense like coiled springs. Half of the top of his head is still bald. Only one horn has started to grow back and that one's not much more than a stump.

I wait for the right moment, when he's totally immersed in his ritual. Balzuzu kneels again. He spreads his arms wide summoning the next tainted soul to become part of him, one of the unlucky 666. The one closest to me responds to his command, swiftly changing direction, darting down towards him.

I do the same.

It's a quick jump. The 'soul drop' lands on his head. My feet land on his broad shoulders. Then before he can react to what's happening, I spring forward, dive over the top of his skull and simultaneously thrust a dagger into each of his eyes. The sharp blades slice deep into his squishy orbs. Eye fluid gushes out, squirting onto my hands. It reminds me of the time I sloppily gutted my first trout, only I don't feel bad about this. My momentum carries me forward. I tuck my chin into my chest, turn my dive into a full somersault, and hit the slimy floor of the cocoon feet first. After a proud glance back at my achievement, I'm off and running. I just poked the bear. I better be clear before the bear pokes back.

Balzuzu's scream shakes the entire chamber. I scan for the tunnel my brother and I loaded up with C-4. There's no way to know for sure, but directionally I guess it's the exit furthest from where I am. I don't second guess myself. I don't have the time. Still, before I enter it I can't help but stop to admire my handiwork. Life's just too damn short not to relish this moment and this very well could be the last thing I see. It's worth every penny. Balzuzu's blinded, swiping wildly at the air, rampaging in his black bath like a mindless gorilla. It's a Kodak moment if ever there was one. I smile, taking it all in, locking it forever in my memory, hoping my brother is somewhere close enough to see it as well.

Then Balzuzu settles down and pulls both knives from his sockets. My jaw drops as one dagger comes out with his eyeball still attached. I haven't enjoyed watching something this much since the Barbarella twins put on a private sex show for me in

Bangkok. I'm mesmerized. He's like a train wreck I can't take my eyes off of. I backpedal the rest of the way to the tunnel, knowing I'm not exiting stage right until he sees it was me. I want to look him in his one remaining eye and get the satisfaction that comes with him knowing I got in one good shot. I'm mental that way. It takes him a few seconds, but finally he spots me. I'm grinning ear to ear like Bugs Bunny.

"That's for my family, asshole," I yell.

He's seething with rage, looking uglier and nastier than ever. I've seen that look many times before. I tend to have that effect on people.

"Silas Hill." He snarls. "Your family is about to end. I will destroy them. I will ground their feeble bodies into primordial paste. *But not you.* Your fate is going to be special. Your soul may be too pure to belong to me, but your body is another matter. I will keep you here and pin you to my wall. You will be my personal plaything. I will skin you alive. I will burn your extremities. I will take pleasure as I remove your teeth one by one. I'm going to torture you in ways you cannot even imagine, relishing in your screams of agony for years to come. Then I'll dismember your body while you still live and feed your meaty little limbs to my dog and pin your eyes open so you have to watch while he gnaws on your bones."

I grin even wider. "Yeah, well good luck with that considering I fed your little poochie a mouthful of hand grenades and turned him into pepperoni road pizza." His anger kicks up a notch as his one good eye registers what I said as the truth. "Don't worry," I add. "I'm sure you could adopt another one at the three-headed monster shelter down on Fuck You Street." I throw in a double middle finger just in case my message wasn't clear.

He snorts irately and there's no more need for words. I flee into the tunnel like a lightning bolt and he bolts after me. He careens off the floor, out of balance. I can't tell if it's his damaged wings that are disorienting him or if losing an eye has thrown him off-balance. Either way, I don't give a shit. I'll take any advantage I can get. I'm run at breakneck speed, an all-out sprint for survival. This would be as good a way to die as any, but I'd rather make it out of here alive.

He's a few seconds behind me, flying so sloppily he keeps smashing into the rock walls, occasionally smacking his head on the roof. He looks like a drunk pterodactyl. I grip my remote detonator. I race past the first set of explosives and press the trigger that activates the blasting caps. Within a few seconds a loud boom thunders behind me. Black rock collapses from above, blocking his way. Balzuzu takes less than two seconds to power his way through it. I don't stop running. Despite his awkward flight pattern, he's closing fast. But my brother spaced the charges well. I'm already racing by the next pairing of C-4.

I press the trigger again.

The boom is louder this time, the blast more effective. Something shifts, as whatever passes for a fault line in this cave takes a hit and the whole cocoon starts shaking like a 6.0 on the Richter scale. I stumble. My hands catch the ground supporting me. I stand erect and keep running as rocks collapse behind me in a boulder-sized hailstorm. One smashes the ground at my heels and spatters me with debris, but I'm not complaining. I'm still hauling ass while Balzuzu's the one in need of an umbrella. I watch him take the brunt of it. He whacks the first few boulders away as easily as if they were flies, like a giant slapping a baseball. Unfortunately for him, the sky is falling. A stone the size of a Volkswagen crushes the side of his head. Balzuzu falls, yet there's no let up. The hits keep on coming, burying him under a ton of rocks and massive black stones. This day just keeps getting better and better. I smile like it's Christmas morning. But I keep running.

An earthshaking roar echoes through what's left of the tunnel followed by the sound of his powerful fists pounding on stone. The one-eyed fuck is nothing if not resilient. I swear I could drop his whole house on his head and he'd still be kicking. I pass the last two charges, the ones we set closest to the entrance and decide to put my theory to the test. I slip behind the nearest stalagmite, hoping it's thick enough to shield me. Then I press the detonator that adds to the mess.

The explosion is massive. A shockwave blasts forth sheering off the top half of the stalagmite I'm hiding behind. My left eardrum pops. I duck lower as mini debris showers over me. An opaque cloud of thick dust pillows outward blocking out what little light there is the way volcanic ash blocks out the sun. I cover my nose and mouth, get low, and hold my breath as dark ash colors my exposed skin.

After about a minute, it subsides. I peek up and see the bang I got for my buck. The front side of his cocoon fully imploded, leaving Balzuzu under a mountain of rubble, fully burying him in the remains of his own home. I hope it's his final resting place.

He wanted to put the human race six feet under. Now he's fifty feet under and Hell can be his silent tomb.

I linger, doubting he's truly dead, even under all that weight, but perhaps being buried alive is a fate worse than death. It's a fate I wouldn't wish on my worst enemy. It's a fate the evil prick deserves. Satisfied, I stroll to the bike and stand it upright. I rev the engine and take one last look around. Hell is indeed a horrible place; a barren wasteland where's there's no hope, no escape, and you're eternally subject to the whims of these psychotic Nephilim whose sadism knows no bounds. All I can hope for is perhaps I at least gave my brother a temporary reprieve.

I spin the bike, a skid of rubber marks my turn. It's time to leave this awful place. Then the mountain of rubble that was Balzuzu's cage rumbles. Stones vibrate, shutter, and slip aside as what's buried beneath them shifts, moves up, rises. I stare, disbelieving. A thick red hand pushes through the debris, similar to the way the zombies rose from their graves. Then Balzuzu bursts free of the stone pile like a dragon emerging from the water.

I am so going to die!

28

Balzuzu roars so loud I can't even hear the roar of my bike as I gun the engine. People say evil never dies, it can only be contained. After witnessing what I just saw, I think they're wrong. Balzuzu is the personification of all things evil and he's irrepressible, unstoppable… a juggernaut of bad news that never stops coming. We hit him with missiles and mountains, yet we barely slowed him down. I've killed a lot of monsters in my travels; vampires, mummies, golems. Balzuzu's completely different. He's a universal force, the darkest of the dark side of nature. I don't think there's anything on this planet short of a nuke that could stop him and even that would probably only slow him down for a week.

There's nothing left for me to do but get the hell out of here—pun fully intended—and hope I can somehow avoid an excruciatingly painful death. I realize now that Miguel was right; voluntarily going to hell was a monumentally stupid idea. Sure I got some great licks in on the embodiment of evil. And it was great to chat with my brother again. Those things were immensely satisfying, but I didn't just poke the bear, I poked the devil and he's not someone that just pokes back. He rips, tears, mutilates and utterly destroys. I should have just let Miguel close the gate and fought whatever evil there is topside where I can deal with it.

I got the bike doing eighty heading straight for the portal. Balzuzu's on my six doing a wobbly eighty-five, screaming like a banshee, never letting me forget how hopeless my situation is. Because even if I make it, even if I outrun him, then what? I won't survive the trip back without my thermal suit, which I too casually discarded. I guess it's better to die in a burst of flame, let my soul sail off to heaven, than to be Balzuzu's eternal plaything. But I know he'll still kill my family and make my brother suffer a thousand years of torture.

"You will not escape, Silas Hill," he screeches.

I wince. Not only because he's using my full name like a scolding mother but also because I can tell by the volume of his voice that's he's close behind me. My brother thought this may happen. He figured the cocoon charges we planted might not do the job. So first he helped me prepare an exit strategy. The latter half of the C-4 went into the cocoon tunnel. The first half we laced along my pathway home, the same way terrorists lace the roads with IED's. I swerve left between two large stalagmites, the first of the landmarks we marked. Balzuzu follows my path. I hit the detonator, exploding the pillars of stone. The flame and pelting debris don't do much to him, but they do afford me a little extra distance.

"Was that a joke, Silas?" he taunts. "Your last feeble attempt to prevent the inevitable?"

I ignore him. I swerve right. There are two more stalagmites stacked in front of me, one to my left, and one to my right. These are C-4 laced as well, but Balzuzu's not stupid enough to fall for the same trick twice. He simply flies above and around them. I set them off anyway just for the slightest possibility it might slow him down. I think I'm close to the gate. He's trailing far enough behind me where I should be able to make it.

Then I hit a jut in the stone. My motorcycle bounces. The wheels spit black pebbles and something sparks as a part of the cycle's metal frame scrapes against stone. Luckily, I'm able to keep my balance, straighten it out and keep going, except that mini adventure slowed me down. Balzuzu's just spitting distance away. I lean forward and reaccelerate the bike to its top speed, not caring if I completely wipe out on the bumpy terrain.

Balzuzu taunts me again. "You do realize that even if you make it through the gate, I'm coming with you. Only this time I'm not going to conquer. This time, I'm just going to hunt down your mother and rip out her heart. Then I will slaughter your father. Then I will bring you back here so your fate will be exactly as promised."

I don't answer him but he's right. Even if I make it, so will he. And even if I don't burst into flames like a marshmallow in a campfire, he'll capture me and make me watch as he brutalizes everyone I care about. Balzuzu's in the soul game. Before it was just business for him, but I hurt him bad. Not only did we ruin his plans for judgment day, but then I came here, destroyed his home, and took his eye. It was always personal to me. Now I made it personal to him. He'll never stop until he gets revenge.

His voice echoes again throughout the canyons of hell. "But if you stop. If you willingly give yourself to me right now, I promise you, I will spare your family," he says.

A deal with the devil… now I see firsthand how it works.

"Your choice, Silas Hill. You can sacrifice yourself to me to save your family or you can all die horribly?"

It's a tempting offer too, my soul for my ma and pa's. I see the gateway before me, approximately ten seconds away.

Balzuzu's just a few meters behind. If I hesitate even for a second, he'll have me.

"Time to choose, Silas. Die in a burst of flame, knowing I'll be back in your world, knowing I'll kill your parents. Or save them and stay here with me."

He plants his seed of doubt. Fortunately, I saw how well dealing with him worked out for my pa. I take my hand off the bar long enough to give him my answer in the form of my middle finger. If that's my last gesture, so be it. Then I lean forward and pray that my velocity will carry me through the flaming portal before I get burnt to a crisp. Balzuzu shrieks. I pretend it's the roar of a crowd and I'm Evel Knievel. Then I scream like a girl and launch myself into the ring of fire.

The bike plunges into the abyss like a guided missile. The surrounding heat envelops me. But at the velocity I'm going, I make it through before I get too singed. Then the world flips upside down. For a micro-second I'm falling up then the gravity reverses and I'm forced into a hard 180-degree flip by the unyielding law of gravity. The twist is too sharp, too disorienting. I can't hold onto the bike and now I'm falling down, helplessly heading back into the hellhole. My mind briefly registers Balzuzu coming toward me as I'm dropping. His eye narrows as he gleams his prize. His disgusting goat mouth registers a high degree of satisfaction. His fat clawed hand reaches up for my tiny body.

Then there's a flash of light, a quick whooshing sound, and I land hard on the ground, face planting into dirt that wasn't there a second ago. I spit soil and grass from my mouth. I turn my head and I'm looking right into Balzuzu's eye, which is only a few inches from my own. I scream, a gasping aaaah, stand up, backpedal, and stumble right into Miguel's arms. The gateway to Hell is gone replaced by a clear circle of fertile brown soil, the only thing fresh in the middle of this dilapidated graveyard. The top half of Balzuzu's head is laying there, his partial horn jutting up from its amputated scalp. A top row of sharp triangular teeth bite the ground. Next to the empty socket, the one remaining eye stares blankly, devoid of any presence of life.

Miguel releases me. He casually walks over to Balzuzu and gently closes his eye. Then he looks skyward, kneels next to it, and draws a cross on his chest, before bringing his palms together graciously thanking God.

I cautiously approach, shaking the cobwebs from my confused noggin, giving my brain time to adjust to what just happened. "You closed the gate," I say to Miguel.

"Yes," he replies with a nod.

"And Balzuzu?" I ask.

"See for yourself," Miguel says, stepping to the side.

I reach down, grab the severed skull by the horn. "Holy…"

Miguel smiles. "I don't think he'll be bothering any of us for quite a while."

29

We're back in town. It looks like a small war-torn nation. Cars are flipped. Windows are broken. Buildings are empty shells. The town church is merely a remnant. People are wandering about, not sure what to do or where to go, their lives irrevocably altered. Others are more purposeful, rushing to help the wounded, carrying them into triage tents which were erected in my absence on every block.

The National Guard is present doing what they can. The Marines have arrived as well, securing the town's perimeter so no one comes in or out, doing mop up duty making sure every nook and cranny is all clear. In the park, the bodies of the unlucky are lined up awaiting a proper funeral. Across the park it's the opposite, zombie bodies are being tossed in a pit by men in Hazmat suits and burned. The werewolves are gone. Balzuzu's skull top is in my backpack. I ask five people before I get the right answer as to where to find my pa. He's in a medical tent just off Main Street.

We walk inside, pushing aside the canvas flap. It's sparse; a dozen beds, two doctors in lab coats, portable medical equipment. Not bad for short notice. Pa is sitting up in one of the beds getting a drink of water from an overweight nurse. One arm is in a sling. His left leg is bandaged and elevated on a blanket. A soft brace wraps around his neck. He sees us, starts to jump out of bed, and winces as his body reminds him that he can't. We rush over to him before he stubbornly tries again.

"It's over," states Miguel.

Pa looks at us in disbelief.

"We won," I add.

"Obviously," says Miguel, wryly.

"That's impossible. He's too powerful. He'll just come back," Pa says with a shake of his head.

I take my backpack off my shoulders, open it, and pull out the half head. It takes a few seconds before my pa fully understands what we have. I smile knowingly at him. Miguel nods in confirmation. Then Pa smiles and lets out a 'Oorah' that rattles every patient in the tent.

"How did you?" he asks.

Miguel gently places a hand on Pa's shoulder. "Your son literally went to Hell and back."

I shrug modestly. "Seemed like the reasonable thing to do."

Miguel shakes his head.

Pa laughs. "You certainly look like it," he says. "You're a Marine, Silas" he adds.

"I'm a Hill through and through," I respond. I wait a second then sigh in a way that tells my pa something he doesn't want to hear is coming. I know what I'm about to say next is going to be painful to him. "I ran into Christian down there."

My father's jubilation is immediately wiped away. Fear, sorrow, and regret cover his face.

"He's okay," I say. "Tough as ever. He made the best of it. Got in some revenge of his own. He wanted me to tell you he doesn't blame you for any of it. He wants you to forgive yourself."

My pa, one of the strongest men I know, completely breaks down. He weeps, uncontrollably sobbing. I don't know what else to say.

Father Miguel firms up his grip on Pa's shoulder. "Jebediah, it's long past time to let the healing process begin," he says.

30

I spend the night at the house. I wash myself in the shower for over an hour. Father Miguel bunks with me as he has no other place to stay. In the morning, I shower again.

After a hearty breakfast, I pack a knapsack and take a hike through the woods into werewolf territory. I pass a few members of the pack. They eye me, always with a little hunger in their stare… their natural look I guess. But they leave me be. By noon, I reach the main den. Rebel emerges from the cave to greet me. He shows me two rows of teeth which I take for a smile.

"It is good to see you my small friend." He says it with a grin, but I know he doesn't call me that as an insult. He says it with pride. He was like me once and means it as the highest compliment, the littlest guy in the room who isn't afraid of the biggest.

I nod. "You too, my rather large, furry, and quite scary-looking friend."

His paw smothers my hands in one of the most one-sided handshakes I've ever had, and he throws his other arm around me giving me a manly feral hug. "You do our kind true," he says proudly. "Both our kinds."

I nod my thank you. "Where's Silver Joe?" I ask.

At first, he doesn't know who I'm talking about. Then he bellows, "Ha! So that's what you call him. He's inside the cave." Rebel pauses. "He's not in a good way. Balzuzu crippled him to a degree he is not healing properly from."

"That's… unfortunate," I say respectfully. "May I go inside?"

"Of course," Rebel replies. "You are welcome here like you are one of us."

We enter the cave, going deeper in then I did when last I was here. Silver Joe is facing away from us, pacing slowly on a bearskin rug, using a walking stick to keep himself upright.

"You smell much better today than yesterday," says Joe, without turning his head. There's bitterness in his voice, an edge of anger. I understand. He was the leader of his pack. He was strong, proud. Now he's a cripple.

"You paid a heavy price for following me, for betraying Balzuzu," I say.

Silver Joe turns, faces me, snarls. "So you came to thank me," he says, harshly. A bead of saliva drips from his fangs. If he was able to, I'm fairly certain he would lunge at me.

"No," I say. "It was you who started this war. It was you who conspired to free the devil. And let's not forget, you did try to have me killed."

Joe growls. Rebel steps forward, ready to protect me. Not that he had to. My Beretta is already in my hand, aimed straight at Joe's heart, ready to fire a well-placed silver bullet if the need arises. Rebel sees it and smiles. I nod my approval and smile back. Joe backs down.

"So, why did you come?" asks Silver Joe.

"I am a man of my word. I told you to leave the big red fuck to me." I put the gun away, reach into my knapsack and pull Balzuzu's head out by the horn.

"For real?" says Rebel, clearly astonished at my kill.

"About as real as it gets," I answer. I turn to Silver Joe. "You are free… as promised. All of you. Every werewolf is now free to choose his own path." Joe reluctantly grunts his acceptance. I put my trophy back into my pack. "The treaty we have is no longer necessary. The people of Los Agros do not know the whole story. They are grateful for your help. You, any of you, are welcome in town anytime you want. I'm sure you enjoy the hunt, but if there is ever a shortage of game, they would be happy to provide you with supplies and food."

Joe turns away. I've said what I came to say so I turn away as well. As Rebel and I walk away, I stop briefly at the gun rack. My pa's rifle is there, leaning up against the old wood. I take it with me as I leave.

31

It's a week later. I'm at the local pub, The Pile Inn, with my pa and Father Miguel. It's fairly crowded as it's one of the few places that have reopened since the attack. It's been quite popular with both the in-town crowd and the out-of-towners that came here to help us rebuild. We're sitting at one of the round, stained-wood tables in the middle of the room. I chose this table for a reason. It's the center of attention and it has an empty seat.

The waitress comes over, an aging blond named Gladys who's been serving patrons in this establishment since I was a pup. The years and current events haven't dimmed her spirit a bit. Her smile is as wide as her waistline. "Welcome Father, Jebediah. Good to see you again, Silas. Can I take your drink order?"

Miguel answers, "I'll take a Killian Irish Red."

"Make that three," I add.

"Make that two," my pa says. "I'll just have water."

Nice to see my pa's laying off the booze. I give him a nod of approval but say, "Leave it at three. I wasn't ordering for you."

"Oh, I could come back when the rest of your party is here," says Gladys.

"He's here now," I say.

The front door to the pub opens and the room goes silent. Rebel walks in, tall dark and furry, walking upright on his hinds. A Marine by the bar glides his hand carefully to his holster. Martaan's sitting next to him. He grabs the Marine's hand, quietly letting him know not to do anything rash. Rebel steps forward, looking around as every single person in the pub stares at him with either anger, fear, or suspicion.

"How y'all doing?" asks Rebel with a tilt of his snout. He turns to a particularly fear-filled woman. "Evening, Ma'am." Then he strides over to our table and sits down. Gladys is frozen in silence, the smile vanished from her friendly face.

"I ordered you a Killian," I say.

"Haven't had a good brew in ages," Rebel responds.

"This is my pa, Jebediah."

"We've met," says Rebel.

"And Father Miguel," I add.

"A unique pleasure," Miguel responds.

"And the lovely lady to your left is Gladys," I continue.

"Please to make your acquaintance, sweetheart," Rebel says.

Gladys repeatedly nods her head in agreement.

"It's okay. He doesn't bite," I say. "Well, he does bite, but it's still okay."

"Aw, hell," says Gladys. "Caught me by surprise, that's all. And after last week, I thought nothing would surprise me anymore. I'll go get your drinks."

"And this is…" In my head I call him Rebel, but now I realize I don't know his real name.

"Cooper," says Rebel. "Least I was. Is everyone still staring?" he asks.

I look around. Most are still looking our way, but when they catch me catch them looking they go back to being normal. "I think they're over it," I say.

Rebel takes the napkin off the table and puts it in his lap. "Good, then let me see a menu. I haven't eaten a decent dead animal in a week. I'm starving."

The meal goes as planned. I invited Rebel… Cooper… as an exercise in acceptance. The quicker all of us get used to each other, the less chance there is for future misunderstandings. The meal comes. Not surprisingly, Cooper ordered his steak rare. Surprisingly, the conversation was pleasant. Cooper told us a bit more of his backstory. My father recounted some of his tales as a

Marine. Miguel suggested they both need to come back to the church, when it gets rebuilt of course.

Then Miguel goes oddly silent, his eyes open wide, his body frozen, as if he had been possessed. The conversation stops. Our looks become worrisome. Then, just as suddenly, Miguel exhales and is back to normal.

"No need for alarm," says Miguel.

"Okay… then, what was that?" I ask.

"That, my good friends, was God. The devil is not the only one who owns the ability to move souls."

If not for everything we just went through, I would have looked at Miguel like he was one flew over the cuckoo's nest. But there isn't a doubt in my mind that Miguel is telling the truth. I knew in my gut that God just spoke with him.

"He has messages for you," Miguel continues.

"I'm intrigued," says Cooper. "Let's hear 'em."

"Christian is with him now. He was willing to resign himself to eternal torture in Hell in order to thwart the devil's plan. In doing so, he purified his own soul. His actions did not go unnoticed."

Miguel gives Pa and I a moment to let that sink in. The relief in our hearts is palpable. "Thank God," I mutter.

"You're welcome," responds Miguel. "Cooper… Cooper James the second to be precise."

"How did you know? Holy Hanna," Cooper whispers.

Miguel continues, "Christian's path is something you should take note of. You as well took a great risk. For that *He* thanks you. It's a start for wiping your slate clean. What you do with the rest of your days, where your ultimate destiny lies, is solely up to you."

"Well, hot diggity. Thank you, Padre," says Cooper, raising his beer.

Miguel stops talking and takes a bite of his steak as if he has nothing more to say. My pa and Cooper renew their meals as well. I feel like I'm back in recess, the last kid picked for the basketball team.

"And…" I say loudly, drawing it out.

Miguel looks at me, slightly puzzled. "And?" he questions me.

"Doesn't God have anything to say to me? I mean… I did storm through the gates of Hell by my lonesome… against impossible odds, facing certain death I may add. Perhaps a little 'hi' might be in order," I suggest.

Miguel sighs. "Silas, when you fled Hell with Balzuzu about to snatch you, tear you limb from limb I may add, all this past week did you not wonder how I knew the exact moment you were to emerge from the gate? Did you not ponder the odds of my impeccable timing of sealing the gate shut at that precise moment that both ended the threat of Balzuzu and saved your life?"

I gulp. "That was Him." Miguel smiles. I shake my head turning it into a rapid nod as I put it all together. "Okay… that totally works for me. He has my gratitude."

"And you have his," replies Miguel. "Oh, and when you're ready you might find something that interests you in Tibet."

"Tibet? Sure, next stop Tibet," I say. "Who am I to argue with God?"

My pa lifts his mug of ice water. "A toast." We lift our beers in agreement. "To Christian," my pa says.

"To the good lord and the good people that do his work," says Miguel.

"To new friends," I say, tapping Cooper's mug.

"To new beginnings," says Cooper.

We clank our glasses together and binge.

32

It's a month later. I'm in bed. It's 2:00 am., my last night here. For no particular reason I don't like to stay in one place for too long. I guess at heart I'm a wanderer that likes to see the world. Tomorrow I'll see where the wind takes me, though I'm not sure I'm ready for Tibet. Maybe if I stop in Fiji along the way.

My clothes and weapons are packed. Balzuzu's head is on the dresser. I'll either bring it with me or mount it on the wall. My bladder's full. It can't wait until morning. I sit up. The room is dark save for the clock and the glimmer of moonlight that seeps through the curtain. I grab a flashlight off the nightstand and flick the switch. The beam hits the ceiling. I lower it and climb out of bed following the thin lighted path. The light reflects off Balzuzu's head. I walk to the bathroom, taking three steps before I realize that there isn't anything on Balzuzu's head that's reflective. I turn fast, alert, startled.

Balzuzu's eyes are open. Both of them.

Then they close.

I nearly wet myself. His other eye is back and somehow he's watching me. If he still had a mouth, I know he would speak to me, threaten me. I grab his head by the lone horn, look for something to put it in. I remove the pillow from its case and throw it in the pillow sack, tying the end in a knot.

Fuck!

Minutes later I'm in the garage, running the hose, mixing cement in a bucket. After sawing off his horn, I drop Balzuzu's head into the bucket, watch it slowly disappear into the gray gooey ooze then sit there for three hours until it dries. I'm so afraid to leave it unwatched, I pee right there in the garage into an empty beer bottle. The bucket weighs around thirty pounds. As I pack the car I take it with me. I toss it into the front seat of my Mustang so I have eyes on it at all times and drive. I don't say goodbye.

I drive for twenty hours straight, stopping only for gas and to go to the bathroom and when I go the bucket comes with me. I eat in the car and get my food from the drive thru. I arrive at the docks and wait by the gate, refusing to even nod off for a quick nap. A friend of mine runs a freighter that transports cargo across the Pacific all the way to Korea and Japan. He opens up at four in the morning. Takes all morning to load his cargo. By early afternoon, I'm sitting on his deck as we're pushing out to sea.

The bucket goes with me everywhere. The captain finds me an extra cabin below deck. He arranges it so someone in his crew brings me my meals. I only leave the cabin to go to the bathroom and, once again, the bucket always comes with me. I'm sure my behavior looks odd to the rest of the crew, but my friend knows me well enough to keep them away from me and he doesn't ask questions. I keep myself awake for another 24 hours because I know I won't ever sleep again unless I'm one hundred percent sure.

At almost the three-day mark without sleeping or showering, I'm ready. I carry the bucket up to the main deck. A deckhand is watching me.

"How deep?" I ask him.

"Rough guess… two miles," he answers.

Good enough. I pick up the bucket, rock it back, and fling it overboard. It floats on the surface for a moment then slowly disappears beneath the murky sea. Still, I fixate on the spot, making sure it doesn't somehow reappear above the water, until I can no longer see it because the ship moves out of distance. If that evil fuck really is still alive, his head can sit in a cement block, staring into cement at the bottom of the ocean for all eternity. Some people, some monsters, truly get what's coming to them.

I make it back to the cabin, my mind barely at ease, and fall asleep.

THE END... Silas Hill is back, in the Orient, getting into more monster trouble. His next adventure will make your BLOOD COLD. Available now!

Author's Note

My goal when writing any story is to have fun. I've written many characters, and love them all, but Silas is my favorite. Out of the gate he took on a life of his own and, literally, he changes the direction of his own adventures. I especially enjoy writing him and Cooper together because who wouldn't want a scary as heck, wisecracking, bad-ass werewolf as their best friend?

So, whether these books sell well or not, I plan to keep writing more Silas Hill stories. I hope you enjoyed Blood Cold. There are many other books out there on the market for you to choose from. My sincerest thanks for choosing mine.

Acknowledgments

I want to thank Mark Roselle for designing a kick ass cover and Amy Weisbard Bloom and Christine Gabrielson for their invaluable input and support. I couldn't have done this without them.

About the Author

Allan Burd writes in all genres. High concept sci-fi and monster stories are his wheelhouse. His other novels include "The Roswell Protocols", "Blood Cold" (Silas Hill Book 2), Roswell vs. Hell (Silas Hell Book 3), and "Hellion". His children's books include "The Crazy Invisible Kid vs. The Eye Monster" and "The Adventures of Little Al - The Lie". His short stories can be found in "Even in the Grave", "A New York State of Fright" and other anthologies.